THE CUCKOO'S SONG

Short Stories

AMRA PAJALIĆ

Praise

First Published in 2022 by Pishukin Press

http://www.pishukinpress.com/
Copyright © 2022 by Amra Pajalić

Cover design: Created using Canva elements

Proofreading: Renée Robinson

Logo design: Cuba DeSilva

For content and trigger warnings please go to www.amrapajalic.com/themes

A guide for international readers: This book is set in Australia, and therefore uses British English spelling. Some spellings may differ from those used in American English. Please see the back of the book for a guide for international readers.

Pre-publication data is available from the

National Library of Australia trove.nla.gov.au

ISBN 978-0-6453310-1-1

Contents

Introduction

This short story collection features stories I have written over the past two decades and are the map that reveal my growth and evolution as an author.

My first publication credit was with *Siege*, a short story inspired by my husband's family and their experiences in the Balkan War of 1992-1995 living under siege in Sarajevo. This story won a competition, was my first publication credit in an anthology and led to my first review mention. My follow-up *Flirty Eyes*, a fictional story based on my first visit to a nightclub when I was twelve, was also published in the same anthology a year later.

These two credits were responsible for me being signed by a literary agent and the publication of my debut, young adult, award-winning novel *The Good Daughter*.

Suicide Watch features my protagonist Sabiha and her Year 10 work experience at a detective agency that didn't make the cut into the published novel.

Writing a book is a long and winding process and to endure to the end I have learnt to trick myself. I develop extracts from my work in progress as short pieces that I submit for publication. These small successes keep me motivated while finishing a book.

In the five years that it took to complete my memoir I wrote and submitted stand-alone pieces that were successfully published: *School of Hardknocks*, *Woman on Fire* and *Nervous Breakdowns* and became chapters in my memoir *Things Nobody Knows But Me* about being raised by a mother who suffered from Bi Polar. This memoir was also traditionally published and shortlisted for a national award.

Chapters that didn't make the book and included in this collection are: *The Choice*, about the forced marriage of a female ancestor and, *The Heart of the Matter*, a fictionalised account mirroring my reality in seeking plastic surgery to compensate for a heart operation scar.

Fragments is a short story extract from my upcoming thriller novel *Time Kneels Between Mountains,* which is the first of a three book trilogy featuring my protagonist Seka Torlak who survives the Balkan War for three years in the besieged city of Srebrenica. *In Treatment* is a story based on the third novel in the Seka Torlak trilogy and is about Azra who is receiving treatment in a mental health hospital after post-natal psychosis. *Friends Forever* is a stand-alone thriller story.

I have also written and published romance novels under a pen name that are no longer in print. The title story in the collection *The Cuckoo's Song* is a love story inspired by my husband's great-grandmother who lost her first boyfriend as a prisoner of war and fought to hold onto hope when there was none to be found. Another romantic story is *Teddy* about a girl who receives a lingerie teddy from a female friend and is forced to re-evaluate their friendship.

My short story publication credits are in the back of the collection. I hope you enjoy this foray into my writing process and a deep-dive into my muse. Happy reading.

For Sofia:
my inspiration
my muse
my strength
my motivation
I love everything about you
and am thankful every day of my life
that I am your Mama.

And to my husband Fikret:
thank you for sharing this magical life with me.

The Cuckoo's Song

I was ten years old when the gypsy fortune-teller told me the day and the hour of my death and I have been waiting since. As the hour draws nearer peace descends upon me. A lifetime of waiting has its own price to pay.

The gypsies followed the fair that came to my hometown every year. When the gypsies came we locked our belongings away. We called them the plague, but at least we only had to endure them for the week of the fair.

I went with my older sister, Cosima, and her husband, Lorenzo, to the fair. As we got closer the noise got louder. There was shouting, a band playing loudly and the noise from the rides and the screams of those riding them. On the street were many stalls with people selling jewellery, knitting, preserves. I looked at everything with wide eyes, my hand in my pocket as I smoothed the coin my father had given me. In the spaces between the tables beggars sat on the ground, their eyes on the ground as they pleaded for money. We passed a gypsy woman with a young girl on her lap, the child's arm burnt and twisted.

'They do that to their children,' Lorenzo told me. 'It's how they get pity and earn a few lires.'

I gasped, my eyes glued to the child's arm.

The gypsy woman heard him, her face hardened and her eyes flashed her ire. Lorenzo met her gaze and hurriedly walked away. I followed Cosima and Lorenzo, still thinking about the gypsy woman and her child. They had looked hungry and tired.

I ran back to the gypsy woman. 'Here.' I thrust out my coin.

'Thank you my child,' she said, taking it. 'You have done a great deed for me and my child.'

I tried not to stare at her daughter but was helpless not to.

'I too will do you a great deed.' She gripped my hand and pulled me to her. Her hot breath tickled my ear as she whispered against it.

I stood and looked into her eyes. They were blacker than coal and bitterer than pepper. I tore away and ran, terror making me fleet-footed and nimble as I weaved through the crowd, the gypsy's whispers echoing in my head.

A hard hand gripped my shoulder, making me shriek. 'Where are you running off to?' Cosima slapped me on the shoulder. She took hold of my hand and roughly pulled me back to Lorenzo. 'Father told you not to run off without us or he'd give you the belt.'

I started sobbing and huddled against her side.

'It's all right.' Cosima smoothed my hair. 'I won't tell Father.'

For the rest of the night I stayed glued to my sister. Each time Lorenzo reached for Cosima I pulled her toward me, forcing him to walk apart from us.

'I didn't let the brat come so she could keep me away from my wife,' he muttered.

'Lorenzo,' Cosima said with her sweet voice. 'She misses me.'

My sister had married Lorenzo a few months before and moved away. This was her first visit as a married woman and she'd lorded it over me since she came, making me do her washing, brush her hair, make her bed. All the things she'd forced me to do when she'd lived at home but that I'd had a reprieve from when she married.

With the gypsy's words a faint echo, guilt bit me like a wasp. I'd been wishing for my sister to leave and never come back again and according to the gypsy, my wish would come true.

Cosima packed a few days later and I watched her every move. 'Are you happy with Lorenzo?' I asked.

'What a silly question,' Cosima admonished as she folded Lorenzo's shirt.

'Does he hurt you?'

Cosima looked at me. She sighed and sat on the bed. 'Come here.' She patted the bed beside her and when I sat, she put her arm around me. 'You've probably heard noises at night.' Her face turned pink and she avoided my gaze.

'This is what a man and woman do to make a baby. It sounds like it hurts and it does hurt the woman a little bit,' she shrugged.

'But it's a welcome pain because it means that I could have a baby.'

I looked at her with scorn. 'I know how a baby is made. A man puts his pippy in the woman's—'

Cosima clapped her hand over my mouth. 'If you know then why are you asking your silly questions?'

I pushed her hand off my mouth. 'Does Lorenzo hit you?'

'Of course not.' Cosima didn't meet my gaze as she continued packing.

'When are you going to visit again?' I asked.

'Are you ready?' Lorenzo asked as he entered.

'Yes.' Cosima kissed me on the cheek. I latched onto her hand and held it tightly. I started crying, my mouth open and snot dribbling onto my lips.

'You'll see me again soon.' Cosima pried my fingers off her.

I shook my head, not letting go.

'When I have a baby you can visit and help me take care of it.' Cosima patted my hand and went to Lorenzo. He put his arm around her and led her outside to their car.

I watched through a veil of tears as she left. I tried to run after her but my father held me against him. It was the last time I saw my sister. She'd twisted in the seat and was looking out the back window, smiling and waving as she drove away to her death.

The cuckoo clock rang, bringing me back to the present. As the cuckoo bird popped out of its house thirteen times and trilled its high-pitched song I sat up heavily and pushed myself off from the sofa. My youngest daughter was coming and bringing the grandchildren to visit me. For the next few hours my house would be filled with noise and laughter as my eight year old grandson and six year old granddaughter told me all their secrets.

When I greeted my daughter she looked tired and drawn, closer to my age than to her own forty eight years. I clucked my tongue as I hugged her. 'No good,' I said in my broken English. 'Look like old woman.' In my day we'd had our children young and spent our middle age in peace. I'd had all six of my children by the time I was thirty years old.

'I know Ma,' my daughter said, her forehead wrinkling so that she was the spitting image of what Cosima would have looked like, had she lived.

The gypsy's words had faded over time and I no longer feared her predictions, but in my sixteenth year her words proved true. I spent my days after completing my chores sneaking away to be with my love, Marco.

Marco was a neighbour's son and we'd secretly loved each other since we were twelve years old. We were going to be married when the wretched war ended. It was already the fourth year of harsh deprivations that had stretched everyone's endurance to snapping point.

We'd meet in the cornfield at the edge of our property. Lying side by side we talked about our dreams.

'Australia is the place for us, Francesca,' Marco said, holding my hand. 'It is the land of opportunity.' He lifted my hand to his lips and pressed a kiss there, his gaze still on the bright sky above us.

I turned my head and watched his profile. My Marco was strong and determined. Whatever he put his mind to he achieved. Even in this time of hardship his fields produced the most crop and he always had a little extra food to give to my family.

I kissed his cheek. His eyes focussed on me and he smiled. I leaned over his chest and kissed his lips. He kissed me back for a moment, before pushing me away.

'No, Francesca,' he said as I continued kissing him.

'But I don't want to wait.' I pressed my breasts against his chest. My parents didn't want me to marry while the war was on and Marco agreed with them. I was the only one who thought waiting in this time of uncertainty was crazy. 'The war could last forever,' I murmured against his lips.

For a moment he weakened and kissed me back with all his pent up desire. My heart raced as I felt his need against my thigh, his strong hands gripping the back of my head as he devoured my lips. He wrenched himself away and stood, offering his hand to help me up. 'The war will only be a few more years.'

'A few more years,' I shouted. I slapped his hand away and pushed through the corn, walking home in a snit.

'Such passion,' Marco teased. 'You will scorch the sheets on our wedding night.'

'There won't be a wedding night,' I shouted over my shoulder, not breaking my stride. Marco's laugh wrapped itself around like me like the warm tendrils of a summer breeze.

This was our little game. I knew the next time I saw him Marco would have a gift, a flower or an apple, to give to me as he sweet-talked his way back into my good graces.

Except, there would be no next time. When I came home that day there was a visitor and my life changed.

My daughter walked into the living room carrying a box. 'Look what I found in the bedroom.'

'I was cleaning,' I said as I watched her rifling through the box.

'You should put some of these out in frames.' She caressed a yellowed black and white photo of a man in a soldier's uniform, stony-faced as he started down the camera. 'Have some reminders of Dad around you.' She handed me the photo.

'I have memories here.' I tapped my head. 'I don't need this.' I put the photo back in the box and handed it to her. 'You take and put in frame.'

She looked uncertain.

'Take, take,' I insisted.

She put it in her bag. 'I'll pick out a few and bring the rest back to you.'

I didn't say anything. I had already left all my photos and memorabilia to her in my will. She was the fairest and most sentimental of my children and I knew she'd be the one who'd divide them fairly among her other siblings.

❧

I'd walked into my parents' house rosy-cheeked from my fight with Marco, grass sticking to my dress and legs from lying on the ground. There was a soldier in the living room and my parents' faces were sunken with worry. It was never good to find a Black Shirt in your house.

'Hello Francesca,' the soldier said.

My eyes widened. How did he know my name? Fear blurred my vision and it took me a while to recognise him as Lorenzo, my sister's husband. 'Cosima,' I whispered, looking around for my sister.

My mother sobbed and I saw she was holding a bundle of rags in her arms. As she cried, her arms tightened on the bundle and it let out a shriek. I walked to my mother and saw the screaming red face of the baby she gripped. Mother told me my sister had died bringing her daughter into the world.

Lorenzo took the baby from my mother and placed it in my arms. 'Here is Cosima,' he said, as my hands curled around the squirming bundle.

I looked down at the baby and saw Cosima's eyes looking at me.

'It is time for you to keep the promise you made your sister,' Lorenzo said. 'You promised you would help her take care of her baby.' He took something from his pocket and gripped my hand. 'And now you have to keep your word.'

I felt something cold slide onto my finger and looked down to see my sister's wedding ring on my left hand. My legs gave out. The gypsy's burning black eyes filled my vision and I heard her whispered words once again. 'You will marry your sister's killer,' she had told me and within a week, I did.

The cuckoo bird started singing to mark the fourteenth hour of the day. As it jumped out of its house my grandchildren watched enthralled and counted its cuckoos.

'One, two, three.' The cuckoo's song died. 'Ohhhh,' my grandchildren exclaimed their disappointment and watched as it continued leaping out if its house mutely.

My grandson peered at the shelf above the heater, his index finger pointing at the clocks as he counted under his breath. 'Mum, why do old people have so many clocks?'

'Because we are marking the time left to our death,' I said.

'Mum, don't be morbid,' my daughter snapped. 'Because they like the sound that clocks make.' She told my grandson.

'We will all die.' I placed my hand on hers. 'It is nothing to be afraid of.'

'Don't talk like this.' My daughter gripped my hand briefly. 'You're going to live forever.'

I shook my head. 'No.' I tried to find the words to make her understand. 'We all have a time to live and a time to die,' I wanted to tell her, but even after fifty years of living in Australia, the English words would not trip off my tongue.

By the time I had remembered the English words she was already lost in the tide of life, rushing to separate her children as they slapped and screamed at each other. I smiled. She would learn, just as I had to learn.

While knowing that I would live a long life made some burdens easier to bear, it made others intolerable.

'She must be at least three months old,' I said to my mother as I changed baby Cosima. Mother fearfully looked around to see if Lorenzo was nearby. 'If Cosima died in childbirth, why did it take three months for him to come here?'

Mother didn't answer. She took Lorenzo's dirty uniform out to wash, her eyes flashing her warning. After the uniform was dry Mama took the cast iron out and started ironing.

'I'll do it.' I took the heavy iron from her hands. I pressed the iron onto the shirt and moved it. The iron stuck to the shirt, slightly singing it.

Mama winced. 'You have to do it gently.' She instructed me as I slowly ironed.

I was hanging the shirt on a coat-hanger when Lorenzo entered. He looked at the shirt, noticing the singe on the front pocket. His arm arched back and his face contorted into rage and hatred. I flinched, closing my eyes as I waited for him to strike. He struck, his hand glancing off my head as if he attempted to swerve at the last moment. I opened my eyes.

'Do better in future,' he snapped, and took the shirt away.

Mama hugged me and we both trembled against each other in terror. Is this what my poor sister had to contend with?

The mailman arrived the next day. The mail was sporadic in this time of war, arriving every two to three months. He handed me an envelope that was creased and torn, as if it had travelled over the whole countryside before it arrived to me. I looked at the writing as the mailman pedalled away and gasped—it was Cosima's handwriting. I ran to the barn and climbed the ladder to the attic where the corn was stored, before opening it.

My dear Francesca,

I have given birth to a beautiful baby girl that I named Violetta. She reminds me so much of you when you were first born with her rosy cheeks and long black eyelashes. She suffers from colic and cries a lot, my poor love. I find myself carrying her around all day, attempting to comfort and soothe her.

Lorenzo has joined the Fascists and is serving our beloved leader Benito Mussolini. He is under a lot of pressure as a soldier, trying to prove himself in this time of division to make our country whole. He gets frustrated with my lax housekeeping and says that my ironing of his uniform is inadequate. I remember how your little hands are so deft and careful as you ironed Papa's good suit for cousin Piera's wedding.

Please promise me you will come. I need you so much.

Your loving sister,

Cosima

Now I knew what had happened. Lorenzo must have used his brute strength and struck her. Struck her hard enough to kill her. I closed the letter and cried. If only I had received it earlier.

I held out against my parents' entreaties for a week, attempting to find a spare moment to speak to Marco, but between my parents' watchful eyes, Cosima's demanding screams and Lorenzo's suspicious gaze, it was never to be.

The Black Shirts held the power of life and death in their hands, and in the end there was only one choice to be made. I lost my virginity in the bed that I'd shared with my sister, keeping my eyes closed as my lips formed Marco's name. The next morning I left my sleeping husband and went to the cornfield to meet my love.

Marco sat on the ground and didn't look at me as I sat beside him.

'I didn't want to do it,' I said to his profile.

'I know.' He still didn't look at me.

'I had to because of—'

He stopped me by taking hold of my hand. I gripped it tightly, knowing this was the only touch permitted to me.

'I'm joining the Partisans.' Marco let go of my hand.

'No,' I said. 'You promised you wouldn't leave.'

'Yes and you promised you would be my wife.' His smile was bittersweet.

I covered my mouth as I cried. 'I'm sorry,' I gasped between sobs. 'I'm sorry.'

He leaned over and kissed me on the forehead. 'So am I,' he whispered as he left.

I prayed for death as the gypsy's words taunted me with the knowledge of the years that stretched ahead of me, but even as the war raged around us and many died, I was immune.

I thought that losing Marco was the worst thing that could happen to me, but in my seventeenth year I was to learn different. That was the year that I lost Cosima for the second time.

The fever I thought was from teething carried her away in her sleep. She was thirteen months old when she died of measles and joined her mother. I wrapped her in her mother's wedding dress and we buried them next to each other.

'Don't worry, Bella,' an old woman said after she offered her condolences to my parents. 'You will have your own children soon.' She patted my stomach.

I flinched from her touch, thinking about the children I would have. Children that would have Lorenzo's black wiry hair instead of Marco's chocolate-brown eyes.

I was in my bedroom after the funeral writing a letter to Lorenzo, who was on the front, to tell him about his daughter's death.

'Francesca.' My father knocked on the door gently and entered. He was fighting to hold back tears.

I turned away from him.

'Marco is missing,' he put his hands on my shoulders. He didn't have to say anything else. I knew that Marco was thought to be dead. My father patted me and left.

I had no more tears left. I closed my eyes and swayed from despair, the grinding pain of so many losses wearing me down.

'Your love will remain lost to you if you give up hope,' the gypsy whispered.

I snapped my eyes open and looked around me, but I was alone. I touched my heart and felt it stir to life. There were many people who had been declared missing and been found again. Just the other week my neighbour Giancarlo had returned to his wife and children after they'd mourned him for a year.

I looked at the letter I had been writing to my husband. I had kept my promise to my sister, now it was time for me to keep the promise I made to my love. I crumpled the letter and started again on a new sheet.

'I'll see you next week, Ma,' my daughter said as I walked her to the door. I touched her face with my hand. When she smiled I felt Cosima with me once again.

'*Uno momento.*' I went to the fridge and removed a container. 'I make meatballs for you.' I handed them to my daughter.

'Keep them here for next week.' She tried to hand it back but I pushed it away.

'It's okay.' I squeezed my grandson's cheeks. 'I know he likes meatballs.'

'Muum.' My grandson put his hands onto the container. My daughter sighed and put it in her bag and I saw the photo of my husband in his uniform again.

I closed the door behind them and lay on my sofa and waited. The empty house sighed around me. The weighted silence interrupted by the ticking of the clocks. I'd had plenty of practice at waiting.

I waited for him every day in the cornfield, holding onto the gypsy's words. She'd been right about so much, she had to be right about this too. He came back to me on a warm summer day in 1943 after the Americans swarmed Rome.

I was lying on the ground, the corn rustling around me as the breeze rifled its branches, when he called my name. I opened my eyes and saw that in the two years since we'd said what we thought were our final goodbyes, he'd grown from a boy into a man. He was gaunt and his uniform hung on him. Later he told me about the two years we lost while he was a prisoner of war.

'Marco,' I said his name like a prayer and ran to him.

He hugged me, before quickly letting me go. 'I have to go.' He started to walk away.

'No, please don't go,' I begged as I clutched at his hand. 'I have so much to tell you.'

He pulled his hand away. 'You will have to tell those things to your husband.'

'No.' I threw myself in front of him. 'I want you to be my husband.' I looked down at the ground. 'As long as you will have a divorced woman.'

I had divorced Lorenzo after baby Cosima's death, while my parents howled their protest. Lorenzo had reluctantly let me go, after I wrote to him what I'd learnt about my sister's death.

Since the divorce I'd become the social outcast of my village and the only thing that had sustained me was the hope that Marco and I would be together. But now that the moment of truth was finally upon me I couldn't look at him for fear of the disgust I would see on his face. He placed something in my hand. I looked down to see an apple.

'I guess we will have our wedding night after all.' He smiled.□

The cuckoo bird fluttered, doing its mute dance fifteen times. The fortune-teller had told me, 'You will die when your hair is grey, when your face is like a dried fig, and when the cuckoo bird stops singing.'

It was time.

Siege

8 September 1992

We are in Ramo's cellar. It seems nearly the whole street is here. We have been here for three weeks now. I think today is 8 September. The days blur into each other as we wait. Sometimes we go for two days without water or a toilet or food.

I am repulsed by our combined smells. The smell of fear, the smell of the slop bucket hidden by a strung-up blanket in the corner, the stench of our unwashed bodies.

We all take turns crouching behind the blanket and then going upstairs to empty our slop out the window. At first we used to avert our eyes when someone made their way to the corner. Now the combined sounds blend in.

The sound of piss trickling into the bucket, or shit dropping down to splatter onto the smelly leftovers from previous visitors. The sound of grenades and bullets wreaking destruction outside. Sometimes it sounds like a rocket-propelled grenade is right over us, that we should expect the roof to cave in on us and crush us to death.

But that is another thing we have gotten used to. We don't flinch anymore when a grenade whistles overhead.

12 September 1992

I haven't seen Darko for a month.

The last time I saw him was at the hospital where he works translating for UNPROFOR. He told me he was going to try to get out through them. He plans on going to Novi Sad where his brother is and then onto Slovenia where he has other family.

He asked me to go with him. I didn't answer him.

We went to his house and made love with frantic desperation. The desperation of not knowing if we would see each other again. For a while our differences were forgotten, the hurtful words we exchanged that day were soothed with our touches and kisses.

Before I left, he asked me again if I would come with him. I looked into his eyes. My first love, my lover of seven years. He knows me, he knows the fear I carry. I could see the hurt I had caused him, and still I couldn't tell him. I couldn't give him the words he needed.

23 September 1992

Nermin received the draft today. He is just seventeen years old but they are calling him up. My baby brother has to go to the army. He hasn't even had the chance to finish high school. He doesn't know anything about weapons or fighting.

He ran away from the house and came back with red-rimmed eyes hours later. After Nermin left Mum started crying too. Father tried to comfort her, but he was holding in his own fear. He hid in the garage for the rest of the day. Ferida and I sat with Mum on the couch, our arms around each other as we sobbed quietly.

I wrote a letter to Faruk. I tried not to worry him and make him feel guilty about leaving, but I had to tell him about Nermin being drafted. It's not his fault that he got out and Nermin stayed. We didn't know what would happen. When Nermin started crying and clutching Mum, our parents let him stay and forced Faruk to leave by himself. Faruk was the oldest and had to be protected. We didn't know that in only two years' time they would be drafting any male up to the job.

29 September 1992

We haven't received any humanitarian aid for two weeks. It's getting scary. There is no minced beef, or potato, or cheese, or spinach to make pita. There is nothing but rice. We have now learnt to make pita by mixing rice with powdered milk and vinegar and leaving it to ferment overnight. This is our substitute for cheese. Instead of spinach we use beetroot leaves. Now we just need to find a substitute for minced beef.

Dad goes to town every day to exchange what little vegetables we have for food. Between giving out onions to the neighbours and the thieves stealing from the garden, there isn't much left.

I'm worried about Darko. It's worse in the city, they have no backyards where they can grow vegetables and are starving. We have heard that people are committing suicide.

The aid stopped when during shootings at the airport, a bullet hit the tail of the plane in which Phillip Morion, the General of United Nations, was flying. Who are they punishing?

1 October 1992

I wrote another letter to Faruk in Austria and sent it through the Red Cross. We're all worried about him, we're worried that he might try to return like so many others did. He can help us more by being outside, rather than being trapped here like we are.

The water truck hasn't come for a while to deliver water. We heard that there is no petrol to power them. Father has been going at night to get water from the well at Ismana's house. Every time he leaves the house, we wonder if he will make it back. Although it is safer at night, we're still scared.

9 October 1992

Darko called today. He was going to meet a food convoy. He didn't say it, but I know he will be trying to get out. He said that he would call. I pray he makes it.

Ramo's cellar was getting too crowded and the cold of winter is starting. We are now in our house. We hide in the small toilet under the stairs when the shelling starts.

We mostly stay in what was Ferida's room. We have put bags of sand nearly to the top of the window, blocking out bullets and sunshine. We can't leave the house because it's too dangerous so we are stuck in this one dark room with each other for company.

We play cards to keep ourselves amused. Ferida is becoming a regular card shark when she can tear herself away from her textbooks. She is still studying for her exams. I guess it at least gives her something to do. Although I wonder if it's futile, if they will hold the exams at all.

I am studying from my German and English books. As a refugee it would be good to know another language.

We irritate each other in this small space.

Father has the radio on all day. We have used up all the batteries we had, first the batteries from the remote, then the calculator, then we boiled and re-boiled them all. Now the boiling of batteries doesn't work anymore. We got the battery from the car and are trying to ration our listening.

Once that is finished, we will be cut off from outside news. Although who knows, that might be better than listening to the lies. At least Zagreb Radio lies less than Serbia radio.

Since winter started we wash our hair in a bowl and bathe once a month. We have some firewood left from summer, but there isn't enough to last the whole five months of winter. We were forced to use our supplies to cook in summer because there was no electricity.

According to the official news on the radio there is no artillery action. UNPROFOR only record grenades sized 150 millimetres and up. I guess snipers and heavy machine-gun fire aren't worth recording. It's not as if they can kill us.

15 October 1992

Mum is sick. Nermin comes home for seventy-two hours and then goes again for forty-eight hours as a lookout. She watches him with frantic eyes. When Nermin leaves she can't sleep and watches the door, waiting.

When he comes home, she clutches at him. She isn't eating much. She puts her share of the food aside and tries to share it among us. But she saves the most for Nermin.

He is changing. I can see it in his eyes. He took the Metallica emblems off his jacket so Mum could sew on the Bosnian's army emblem, the Golden Ljiljan. He's carrying the Koran with him, and he was the one who was the least religious of all of us. We are scared to ask him about what he sees.

They are talking about negotiations on the radio. But it's all a lie. Negotiations or no, we are still getting bombed every day. After every negotiation ends, or a cease-fire, they bomb us even more ferociously.

23 October 1992

In the city all the trees are cut. People are now reduced to pulling out stumps to collect firewood for winter. Everything looks so bare. They said on the radio 'Sarajevo's trees are dying so that people can survive.'

They have run out of burial room at the Lion's cemetery. Now they are burying people in the athletic track at the stadium. I guess Sarajevo will always have its fame. Once it was for the Winter Olympics of 1984, now it is for the war of the Balkans. I guess the dead will provide company for the ghosts of the Olympics.

They can't hold burials during the day. We provide easy targets for snipers. Now all burials take place at night.

2 November 1992

Joke from the radio:

Do you know the motto for the Serbian Pacifist Party?

Serbia all the way to the Pacific.

7 November 1992

We heard through the grapevine that they are distributing help again. Ferida and I went to the city. Snipers were in good form. It took us three hours to make a trip that took twenty minutes in peacetime. It was worth it. Each member in the household received: 300 grams soy flour, 500 grams corn flour, half a litre of oil, one soap for clothes, tin of fish 400 grams, tin of beef 450 grams.

11 November 1992

We sent another letter to Faruk. This is the third letter we've sent. So many others have received responses from family members outside the country. Our biggest fear is that he has tried to return. This time we sent it through the ADEH French Humanitarian organisation.

The phones are cut off and I can't call Darko's friends to see if he made it through. I've been sending letters but I don't know if they will arrive.

In the letter to Faruk I wrote the phone numbers of Darko's friends. I'm hoping Faruk will be able to call them and find out where Darko is.

25 November 1992

I dreamt about Darko again last night. It was the night he asked me to marry him. In my dream I said yes. His face lit up with joy.

He said to me, 'Bahra, I will always love you.'

Then I woke up.

1 December 1992

We have had two weeks of peace. The sun is shining, the kitchen is redolent with tasty smells as Mum bakes, and cooks, and bakes. The luxury of sitting down at a table and eating dinner like a normal family cannot be equalled. For a few minutes we are human beings, not bottles lined up for target practice.

Dad fell off the roof. He's okay but he hurt his hip. He was up fixing the last of the artillery damage. Soothing the cracks on the rent surface like a father soothing his child. It took him twenty years to build this house, a brick at a time.

It should not matter so much, a house compared to a limb or a life. But it does.

9 December 1992

They've started again.

16 December 1992

I think about what would have happened if I had said yes. Would I be here now? As Darko's wife I would have been able to get out with him. My family would have been unhappy, but now, with the war, it all becomes unimportant.

I wrote to him. I told him I was sorry I let fear get the best of me. That I was too scared of what my family and friends thought. After I wrote the letter, I placed it on the fire.

22 December 1992

It's New Year in a few minutes. I wish for Darko to be safe and happy, even if it is without me. I wish for Faruk to be well. I wish the war will end soon and everyone will be okay.

I wish I will see Darko again.

10 January 1993

I haven't heard from Darko for three months now. I am hoping that he got through the blockade, that he is somewhere where he doesn't fear daily for his life.

It's hard not knowing. Chances are if he didn't make it, I will never find out. He will just become another body that litters the countryside.

We haven't had coffee for five months. We grind the rice we get from humanitarian aid and pretend it is real coffee. I can't remember the taste anymore.

19 January 1993

Ferida and I returned from the city. We went to where the supermarket used to be, they are now distributing humanitarian aid there. We used to go there to buy food, now we go to beg.

I don't know what's worse. To be hit by a bomb or a sniper, a sniper or a bomb. I guess if I could choose I would rather a sniper's bullet to the brain.

But that doesn't happen very often. They hit Nermana down the street. The bullet ricocheted inside of her and went through her intestines. She has a bag attached to her stomach and is fed through an IV tube.

Ferida has completed two exams for school. She got an eight for Anatomy and nine for Sociology so she can enrol in her third year. We still don't know if school will be held. Her eyes are hurting from studying by candlelight in the shelter. She will probably need glasses when this finishes.

23 January 1993

Father went to the market yesterday to exchange the cigarettes that Nermin gets as payment from the army. He overheard a conversation between two black marketeers. They were saying they had a shipment of coffee but were putting the bags aside in order to make more of a profit later on.

Father attacked them, told them they should be ashamed about exploiting people in these times. One of them pointed to the gun under his jacket and told Father to get lost.

He's hidden in the garage now. Mum is praying. I didn't think she knew how.

28 January 1993

Last night I dreamt I was in Kogo, before the war. I was sitting at our table flipping through *Bravo* magazine. Darko was late as usual so I was catching up on the Hollywood gossip and reading hair and make-up tips. I was staring at a picture of a girl with dark glossy hair styled into a cascade of curls. There were instructions next to the picture about how to replicate the style. I was thinking about how I wanted to buy the brush and styling gel and how Ferida and I would practice doing my hair.

The waitress brought my coffee and placed it in front of me, her hands carefully setting the cup on the table near the edge of my magazine. I didn't look up as she walked away. I reached out and curled my hands around the coffee cup. I lifted the cup to my lips, smelling the dark, heavy scent. The smell hit the back of my throat making my tastebuds crave the bitter-sweet taste in my mouth. I tilted the cup against my lips. The smooth, warm texture slid onto my tongue. And then I swallowed.

5 February 1993

Father spoke to me about Darko today. He asked if I had heard from him. I told him no.

I remember the last time Father mentioned Darko. It was three years ago when he answered the phone and Darko asked for me. He hung up on him and told me that he would never accept a Serbian in his house.

Father told me not to worry. That he could have still made it and just hasn't had the chance to answer my letters.

10 February 1993

We are running low on supplies. Father doesn't feel well so it will be up to me and Ferida to go to the market to exchange the vegetables. I hate the thought of it. Father wouldn't let us go the few times we offered because it's so dangerous.

He's still hoping he will feel better.

17 February 1993

Faruk wrote to us today. He said that he received all our letters and replied each time. He called Darko's friends. They haven't heard from him.

My heart broke. I know now that it is futile.

He is gone.

LIBERATION NEWSPAPER
OBITUARY
23 February 1993
With deep regret the Osmanagić family an-
nounces to our family and friends that our beloved
daughter and sister Bahra Osmanagić was shot
and killed by sniper on 22 February 1993 in Sara-
jevo, aged twenty-six years.

She will be remembered by her bereaved parents
Hanija and Saban Osmanagić, and her siblings
Faruk, Ferida and Nermin.
The funeral is to be held near Olympic Hall Zetra
at 10 p.m. tomorrow night.

Flirty Eyes

When people ask me if I have any siblings I say, 'One, an older brother,' but that's not the truth. I have a sister, or at least I had a sister one summer years ago.

The one thing I remember most about that summer is my sister's 'fuck me eyes.' Not that I knew what that meant, or that I would have thought of that as a description of my sister, but her 'fuck me eyes' were the reason that she lived with us, and the reason that she left.

It was when I overheard a friend of my brother's who described her as 'Fuck me eyes, May' that I realised what her special quality was. I'd just accepted her flirting as an integral part of May. Some people measure their self-esteem by how many qualifications they complete or how many promotions they get, my sister measured hers by the barometer of how many men fell under her spell. She'd get all giggly as she talked about the checkout boy who gave her the once over, or the bank teller who lingered over her notes while he made eye contact, but it wasn't until I heard the comment about her eyes that I started paying attention.

One day we were standing on the corner with the gang. If you knew my suburb you'd know there wasn't anything much to do other than hang around on street corners and shit-stir each other. We'd have to alternate corners because the neighbours in the corner house would get shitty and either threaten us with the hose or the cops, depending on how many kids they had. Mr Motopoulos had no kids living with him so he was the one who'd call the cops, while Mrs Cloone had two sons, one fifteen and one thirteen years old, so she was the hose lady.

It was dusk and we were slapping and scratching our bare skin as the mosquitoes descended. My sister was wearing a spaghetti-strap top without a bra, denim cut-offs that barely covered her arse cheeks and had dangly strings of denim to her knees, and frilly ankle socks with high heels. Sounds weird doesn't it, frilly socks and high heels, yet somehow with her hair tied up with a scrunchy she had this unique look of the whorish schoolgirl.

A car screeched up the street and the tyres squealed as the driver did a burnout. This was a regular occurrence in our street and didn't merit a look but as I was reaching to scratch my shoulder-blade I caught site of my sister. She was standing on the curb staring dead ahead at the driver who was speeding past us. I saw the moment that she caught his eye, his head whipped toward her and their stares locked, then he drove past. Another squeal of the tyres and he did a u-turn, before pulling to a stop by us.

He spoke to one of the guys while staring at my sister. As I watched she looked down at the ground and quickly back up into the guy's eyes. With each drop of her eyes she did a move and drew attention to another asset: a dip of her shoe in the street curb to show off her naked thigh and calf, a scratch of her shoulder which squeezed her unfettered boobs up. By dropping her eyes she gave the guy a chance to check her out yet each time she met his gaze again his attention was firmly back on her face. There was something about her eyes that drew them like bees to honey.

Before this I thought it had everything to do with the package, you know, the tiny waist topped by Baywatch boobs. My sister was pretty close to the ground so even though her boobs were only a C-cup, on her petite frame they came across like a D+. Her height wasn't an advantage only when it came to her boobs, I think there was something about her head never over-reaching a guy's armpit that made her so popular. That whole craning her neck to look up at the big guy seemed to make them feel all manly, and being able to twirl her above their head with one arm made them feel like The Incredible Hulk.

You're probably thinking this sounds a little like sour grapes and I guess you'd be right. Even though she was five years older, I was already one centimeter taller than her at twelve years of age and after that I gained one centimeter to make up for each year of seniority she had on me. Hearing jokes about her in high school made me realise that being May wasn't so cool. Like the one that goes: 'first come the boobs around the corner and then ten minutes later appears May', or 'the advantage of having May as a girlfriend is you can use her breasts as a beer holder,' or

'May doesn't complain about getting a crick in the neck from a blowjob since she can do it standing up.'

But that happened later. At this point, in the summer of my twelfth year, she was everything I wanted to be. We were polar opposites—I was tall, she was petite. I was blonde, she was a brunette. I had blue eyes, she had brown. I was fair-skinned, she had an olive tinge. The first few times we were asked about our lack of resemblance we told the truth and said we were half-sisters. When we received a blank look we had to go into the whole story: she was from our Mum's first marriage, I was from her second, and we both took after our fathers. After a while we learnt not to say anything at all—there were heaps of full-blooded siblings who shared no resemblance.

Watching May get in the car and disappear down the street with the guy made me burn with righteous injustice only a pre-teen can feel as I looked from my bee sting boobs to her udders. As I said, at this point I thought it had everything to do with the package and I thought if only I grew huge boobs in puberty my life would be perfect. Watching my brother's videos and seeing the porn actresses with huge boobs made me think that sex made boobs grow. So I'd started masturbating a few months earlier and was on the way to developing pretty extreme RSI in my right hand.

But when my sister came home that night and I opened our bedroom window for her I started to get an inkling of what her real attraction was. Her hair was out of the scrunchy and all messed up, her t-shirt torn slightly and there were hicky marks on her neck. She took off her t-shirt and denim shorts and I saw what looked like a snail trail on her tits and her belly. I watched as she rubbed it, her face all dreamy.

'He loves me,' she said.

'Really?' I asked as I lay on my stomach on the bed. 'How do you know?'

'If you'd seen his face, you'd know it was true love,' she said, before shrugging into her bathrobe and ducking into the shower.

After she went to bed I opened the drawer to my bedside table and stealthily pulled out my torch and book. Turning the torch on I opened the book to the marked pages. Re-reading the love scenes of the Mills and Boon I slipped my hands into my underpants and fingered myself. The teasing passage and replayed images of my brother's porno fed my erotic fantasies. After I had an orgasm I returned the torch and the book. Remembering my brother's porno I saw again the looks of ecstasy on the men's faces as they came.

'May,' I called quietly. 'How do you know the difference between true love and sex?' Hearing no answer I turned over and went to sleep.

I was to find out over the next few days as she waited for the call that never came that she didn't. While we had dinner and then watched TV in the living room I could see that her ear was cocked for the phone to ring. Each time it did she was off like a greyhound bursting out of the cage, only for her face to drop when the caller asked for someone else in the family.

My father watched her antics with a wary eye. When she left the room for a minute he leaned over and said to me, 'I guess it won't be long before that's your dance, Talia?'

I giggled in delight. He sighed and shook his head, before leaning back in his armchair and switching the channel. Seeing my daddy's face I sat on his knee and gave him a kiss and cuddle. He smiled, the worried frown fading. Hearing the living room door open I turned and saw May had returned. She watched my father and me with an intent look. I slipped off my father's knee and sat next to him to watch tellie, avoiding May's eyes.

As we were getting ready for bed that night May slammed the bedroom door shut after she returned from brushing her teeth. I watched her warily as she shook the doona extra hard. She went to the vanity and put on her face cream. Hearing a crack I turned and saw she'd thrown the plastic tub against the mirror.

'Don't you think you're too old to sit on your daddy's knee, Talia?' she snapped holding my gaze in the mirror.

I left the room to brush my teeth. When I returned she was in bed and the light was turned off. As I sat on the bed I saw myself in profile in the vanity mirror through the moonlight streaming into the room. My boobs were lifting up the t-shirt slightly. I stuck out my chest trying to make more boob.

May had moved in with us after her father and stepmother threw her out and my mum and dad, I mean our mum and my dad, took her in. Up until that summer she'd come to visit irregularly, maybe once a year. What I remember most about those visits is that my brother and I learnt to sneak away from her.

She'd come over to the house and then spent all her time helping Mum clean. If we weren't quick she'd rope us into cleaning our closets and putting away our toys. We used to be jealous because our mum would praise her for washing the dishes or folding the laundry while telling us off for messing up the living room with our toys. For months after she left she'd keep comparing us to May, 'if May were here' or 'May wouldn't do that.'

That year when she moved in I'd twigged onto the value of having a sister. My brother who was two years older had moved onto high school and new friends, leaving me stranded in the band of pre-teen and soon-to-be-teen. With my sister I crossed over that line and learnt about make-up, flirting and clothes. She was the one who noticed when my breasts had developed and took me shopping for my first bra. She didn't buy one of those crappy training bras that were made of nylon with the thin straps, but a flashy lace underwire bra that was the envy of my girlfriends. She was the one who taught me the value of good support in a bra in order to achieve great cleavage. She was also the one who bought me pads when I got my first period a few months before, told me about the dos and don'ts of tampons and what it meant to be a 'woman.' That was when I found out she was a virgin.

It was a Saturday and I had slept in. When I woke I was feeling sluggish, my lower back was aching and my legs were cramping. I ate breakfast in front of the tellie while catching the last half an hour of video hits. On the commercial break I went to the toilet and found blood on my underwear. That's when I connected the sludge coloured watery discharge over the past few months and my budding breasts. After padding my underwear with toilet paper I called May at her girlfriend's house and caught her before they left for the movies. Ten minutes later they dropped off the pads. When she came home that night we sat in the backyard behind the garage. She was smoking while I ate the leftover lollies she'd bought at the movies.

'You know what this means, right, Talia?' she asked as she exhaled. When I shook my head she sighed and blew her fringe out of her eyes. 'If you decide to fuck a boy you, my dear, can now get pregnant. Welcome to the joys of being a woman,' she said as she extinguished her cigarette on the brick garage and threw the butt under the fence where my parents wouldn't see it.

'How come you're not pregnant?' I asked as I chewed the Red Skin I'd dug out of the lolly bag.

'Maybe because I haven't fucked anyone yet.'

My eyes smarted at her sharp tone. She'd never spoken to me like that before. I stopped chewing, the Red Skin sticking to my back teeth as I stared at the ground.

'And if I did I'd go on the pill so I don't get pregnant,' she said as she ran her hand through my hair.

After May left I overheard my mum telling a visitor that May had been thrown out by her father and stepmother because they found a packet of contraceptive pills in her pads.

The visitor sipped her coffee and asked, 'What sort of a mother goes through her daughter's pads?'

My mum looked away without answering and wiped her tears. Even though she was May's biological mother, her stepmother had staked her claim as May's mum by rearing her from the age of five.

The weekend after my period was the first time May snuck out. When she called for me I opened the window to find her holding onto the fence for balance. As I helped heave her through the window I smelt the alcohol on her breath. After taking off her clothes and putting her to bed I found smudged blood on her thigh and underwear. I went to the underwear drawer to get a pad and put it on her night table. Feeling foil under my hands I pulled out a started pill packet and realised that it wasn't her period that was making her underwear bloody.

The next day I eagerly waited for her to wake up so I could ask her about 'IT.' When she woke and saw her thigh, her face changed. When I saw her eyes my stomach went funny. It was like I wasn't looking at May. She looked at me like she wanted to ask a question but couldn't remember what. I made an excuse and left the bedroom, avoiding her for the rest of the day. Her eyes changed after that. It was like she saw something that pushed her onto the outside and she couldn't ever find a way to return to who she was before 'it' happened.

When I came home from netball the next day my mum and dad were fighting. I'd just unlocked the front door and stepped into the hallway when I heard them in their bedroom.

'I don't like what she's doing to this family,' my dad said. 'I don't like the way she's changed everyone.'

I knew he was talking about me. May had taken me to get my ears pierced. When we came home Dad yelled at May and told her she had no right to get my ears pierced without asking permission. Mum jumped in and started yelling at Dad. I stood and watched, my ears burning while feeling like I was going to puke.

'Girls, go to your room,' my dad said, interrupting my mother's yelling.

I started walking off. Seeing that May wasn't behind me I turned around and saw she was staring at my dad without moving. I tugged on her arm and took her to the bedroom. After pushing her in I leaned my back against the closed door.

'Don't challenge me in front of the girls like that,' I heard my dad say to Mum, his voice quiet and scary.

'Who the fuck is he to tell me what to do?' May said really loudly, almost like she wanted my dad to hear her.

I ran across the bedroom and slapped my hand across her mouth. 'Don't,' I begged as I started crying.

May took hold of my hand and pulled me into a hug. When we had dinner that night we all pretended that nothing had happened, but things were never the same after that.

'...is growing up. It's natural for her to change,' I came back to the present when I heard Mum say my name.

'Yes, she is but it's as if she's abandoned her own family for May,' Dad sighed heavily. 'I don't like what's happening with us. We never used to fight like this.'

I remembered what life was like before May. My parents used to sit next to each other holding hands while we watched tellie after dinner. Sometimes I'd catch them kissing each other on the lips, and by the look in their eyes I knew they were going to go to bed early.

'I know you feel guilty about leaving May, but she's not yours anymore. She hasn't been your daughter since she was five years old.'

'That's not true,' Mum said. 'All she needs is to be loved. She's never had that before. I wasn't there to love her.' I heard her crying. 'Please Doug, give it a little more time. Things will settle down.'

I went out the front door and closed it quietly. Counting to five I unlocked the door again and slammed it open with a bang. 'Anyone home?' I yelled.

Dad came out of my parents bedroom. 'Hello, Talia.' He bent to give me a kiss. 'Are you hungry? There's some risotto on the stove.'

When May came home that night I tried to warn her. 'I know your dad doesn't like me,' she said rifling my hair. 'But it's okay, Mum's not going to let him do anything.'

I remembered the look in my mum's eyes at the dinner table as she looked from Dad to May. She looked like the fox I once saw on a doco being hunted by howling dogs but no matter how fast it ran, it wasn't fast enough. In the end there was only one way the doco was going to end for the fox.

In the next couple of weeks my Dad tightened the reins. He wanted to know where we were going and what we were doing anytime we left the house. While I spoke, May stood beside me rolling her eyes or smacking her bubble gum.

⁂

I was sleeping on a Saturday night when I heard her moving around the room.

'May,' I called as I sat up in bed.

'Shhh, go back to sleep, Talia,' she whispered.

The curtains were pulled open and moonlight flooded the room, making me close my eyes. When I opened them she was halfway out the window. 'May,' I yelped.

She froze, sitting on the ledge as we both waited. After a few moments we realised no one had heard. I pushed my covers off and crossed the room, grabbing hold of her arm. 'Come back. If my dad finds out you'll be in deep shit.'

She pried my fingers off her. 'I don't give a shit,' she whispered. 'It's like living in a Nazi camp. I want to have some fucken fun.' Hearing a car she stopped and craned her neck. The car drove past. 'Let go of me. Rick's going to be here any second.'

Seeing her sitting on the ledge halfway to freedom I wanted to be her so badly. Just once I wanted to see what it was like to be admired and flirted with. 'Let me come with you, please,' I whispered, my voice high pitched with excitement.

She stopped and looked at me. 'Okay.' She returned to the room. 'But remember, you have to do exactly as I say.' She rifled through her dresser and grabbed some clothes before jumping out the window. I looked down at my nightie and hesitated in embarrassment. 'Come on,' she whispered impatiently. 'You can get dressed in the car.' With one last look at my bedroom I jumped out the open window.

Rick took us to a nightclub where the bouncer was his friend. When we walked past the line and to the door Rick greeted him without introducing me or May. When we went to enter Rick's friend stopped us. 'Hold up,' he said to Rick. 'What is she, ten years old?'

'No,' May interrupted. 'She's eighteen years old. Show him your ID.' May nodded to me.

I flipped open my handbag and pulled out the learner licence May had borrowed from her girlfriend Rebecca. While Rebecca and I had blonde hair, even though her's was dyed a platinum blonde and splitting at the ends, that was the sum total of our resemblance. Rebecca had brown eyes and was twenty kg heavier than me.

The bouncer looked from the licence to me. I looked away as per May's instructions. She'd told me I had a face that telegraphed guilt when I was lying. From the corner of my eye I saw the bouncer jerk his head for us to enter. I breathed out my relief and took the licence back.

It was my first time in a nightclub and the darkness took me by surprise. May and Rick walked ahead of me. She was wearing a white top and her customary denim shorts, frilly socks and stilettos. The white top and socks glowed under the strobe light. I walked behind them, my feet already aching from May's stilettos. I was wearing her clothes and we looked like twins, except for the lack of any resemblance. My hips hadn't developed yet so I just fit into her denim shorts.

May and I sat while Rick brought us drinks from the bar. I sipped through the straw and nearly choked. Rick winked at me. After doing the whole sickening schmoozy thing with Rick while I pointedly looked away, May led me to the dance floor.

The dance floor was round and it revolved like a turntable. When I first stepped onto it I expected to be sick but it turned so slowly that if it wasn't for the changing men that watched us, I would have forgotten it moved. We didn't even have a chance to start the lesbo moves that we'd practiced at home because with each turn of the dance floor another guy waved May over and we'd get off.

She'd do the whole kissing on the cheeks thing and then they'd talk for a few minutes before she walked away. The conversation would be something like this:

'So cutie, are we going out tonight?' the guy would ask.

'You know I've got a boyfriend,' May answered.

'Oh, come on Babe.' At this point he'd caress her arm, or her shoulder, or her cheek. 'Drop that loser and stay with me.'

She'd giggle and take the drink he was holding and slug back a few sips. Returning the drink she'd say, 'You're so bad,' before returning to the dance floor, her bootie shaking from side to side as the guy watched. Just before she reached the floor she'd turn and look over her shoulder, giving him a flirtatious look with just enough hope so he'd keep trying.

The next time she stepped off I watched the other dancers. That's when I saw him. The guy who was going to be my first. He was wearing all white. This was the time of MC Hammer and the harem pants and this guy was a 'would-be-MC.' He was doing the hip hop moves among a crowd of admirers, mostly women, who jiggled from side to side in their version of a sexy dance. You know the step, shuffle, wiggle. He was ignoring all of them. You could see he was really into the music and almost unaware of everyone else around him.

When May stepped off, I moved away from her reaching hand and kept dancing. I kind of lost myself in the music. I was aware that May returned every few turns and tried to re-engage me in our lesbo moves but I ignored her and kept grooving to my own beat.

I don't know when I became aware that he had noticed me. All of a sudden I looked up and saw his little glance and felt this zing. You know the zing of knowing that a guy is attracted to you. We kept dancing and even though our bodies kept moving to the music, there was an awareness as we slowly moved toward each other. Everyone else was on the peripherals and there was only the two of us and this chemistry as we grooved and bopped.

When we were standing in front of each other we danced slowly, the distance between us disappeared. His hand was on my back, my hand on his shoulder. I looked up and met his eyes and we locked lips. I don't know how long the kiss lasted, it felt like forever and it felt like a second. There was no awkwardness or bumping of noses I had heard about from other girls at school. It was so easy, and so perfect.

Suddenly it was over. May's hard hand on my shoulder wrenched me away. I looked on in confusion as she launched at the guy and started shouting at him.

'What the fuck is wrong with you? She's only twelve years old.'

He looked at me and I saw his face change to disgust. He wrenched his arm from May and left. I watched his retreating back, the fluorescent white disappearing among the weaving bodies on the dance floor. May was talking to me but I didn't hear her. When I came back to earth I realised she was asking if I was okay. 'Did he do anything to you?' she asked, peering into my face. Her mouth smelt of alcohol and her speech was slurred.

I pushed her away and ran. She found me an hour later in the toilet cubicle. When I came out she wanted to say something but I cut her off. 'I want to go home.'

She tried brushing my hair away from my face but I jerked away from her touch. 'Maybe in an hour. Rick is with his friends—'

'I want to go home now,' I shouted in her face.

For a minute, I saw her hurt, but she quickly rallied and stood in front of the mirror. She rifled through her purse and found her lipstick. 'I don't know why you have to be a scaredy baby for,' she said as she applied her lipstick.

I moved to stand behind her. 'Either we go home now or I'll call my dad.'

She met my eyes and looked away. 'Okay, we're going home.' She threw her lipstick back in her handbag.

I saw that her lip-line was crooked but I didn't say anything as I followed her to find Rick. I stood back as she spoke to him. She leaned down and almost sat in his lap as she whispered in his ear. He got up a minute later and walked with her under his arm to the carpark.

When we reached his car he pushed May against it and started kissing and grinding himself against her. 'What are you looking at twerp?' He looked at me as he unlocked the back car door and held it open. 'Go back inside, kid.' He pushed May in. As he went to follow May into the backseat he said with a grin, 'Unless you want to join us.'

'I want to go home,' I said, my voice high and panicky.

'Yeah, well, I'm not ready. So fuck off.' He took a step toward me like he wanted to hit me.

I took a step back. 'May, come on. Let's go home.' I held out my hand to her.

She was sitting on the edge of the car seat, her eyes jumping from me to Rick. 'No. I'm having fun.' She looked away from me.

'May, come on, I'm scared—'

I didn't see Rick move until I was on the ground. He'd pushed me, the unexpected force propelling me until I lost my footing and fell to the ground awkwardly. My palms stung and I'd scraped my knee. Seeing his feet as he approached me I screamed as he lifted me up by the shoulders and pushed me again, with less force this time. 'Fuck off kid.'

I stumbled toward the club, my eyes blurry as I cried.

'I won't be long and then we can go home,' May shouted behind me.

I didn't turn around. The car door slammed shut as I continued walking to the payphone in the club foyer.

In Treatment

'Do you know why you're in hospital?' Dr Russell asked.

'Sick,' Azra forced the English word past her lips.

'Yes, you are sick,' he repeated patiently. 'But what brought you here?'

She knew by his intent manner this question was important. He walked her to the common area and stood next to the television in the corner. It was much larger than the one on the farm. Dr Russell turned the knob. The screen flickered to life.

On screen was the news, reporting a protest in front of Parliament House against the Vietnam War. Azra stared in wonder at the students in their colourful garb and bright banners. The television on the farm was black and white with flickering images that moved like waves.

As they walked back to Dr Russell's office she remembered the day it all began. She was in the kitchen on the farm, washing the dishes when she heard voices coming from the living room. She dried her hands with a tea towel and went to turn off the television. When she entered the living room she stopped abruptly. The television was off, but she could still hear voices coming from it.

'Do you remember now?' Dr Russell asked as he sat back down.

She nodded. 'Hear voices.'

'That's very good.' He picked up his notepad and wrote a note. 'What was the relationship between your parents like?' he asked.

'Fighting.'

'They argued?' the psychiatrist asked.

'No, fight.' She lifted her hand and formed a fist. 'Father hit, Mother hit.'

He nodded, understanding. 'Domestic violence.'

She sighed. A sanitised English word that removed all the brutality of what truly happens when a man lifts a hand to a woman. Her father heaped insults on her mother, cursing her parentage, her very existence as he tried to think of words that would cause the most damage. The way that the house shuddered and cracked as it fought to contain his rage within its walls.

'What is your worst childhood memory?' Dr Russell asked.

The worst was when his hatred spilled to his progeny and he came to the room that she cowered in with her brother and sister. Her mother threw herself in his path, absorbing his blows as she begged, 'Mensur, don't, leave them be.' Sometimes she managed to deflect his attention, but there were times she didn't.

'Father push out house. Cold, snow.' She hugged herself and shivered.

'Your father kicked you out of the house?' Dr Russell pointed at her.

She shook her head. 'Everybody,' she said. 'Mother, brother, sister, me. Everybody.'

'Did you to go a friend's house?'

She shook her head mutely.

'What happened?' He waited. He knew how to use silence to prod her into a confession. The power of his attention, the flattery of him writing down every word she uttered made the words pour forth, a cascading river of shameful disclosures.

'Cold, feet hurt.' She pointed at her foot, curling her toes as she remembered the freezing snow pricking her feet like fire. 'Mum put feet in cow shit.'

He looked concerned. She knew he thought she was drifting into delusional territory. She didn't have the words to describe her mother's look of desperation as she begged her father to let them in. She ran from window to window, knocking and pleading on behalf of her children, while inside he swore, his words slurred from the alcohol he'd consumed.

Mum had wanted to take them to safety, but they had recently moved to this new town seeking work. She didn't have a chance to make any friends, and even if she did it was doubtful she'd seek shelter. There was an unspoken rule among victims of abuse—to make others aware of their plight was to expose their family to shame.

Her mother led them to the manure pile by the barn. She used a shovel to lift the crust of snow. Steam rose in the cold air. She forced them to sit on the pile of excrement and push their feet into the manure. Even now Azra wanted to vomit as she remembered the squishy feeling of manure, the pokes of the straw, and the gooey sound it made. Her mother hugged her children, sharing her body warmth.

'Feet freeze, cow shit warm,' Azra said.

'Frostbite,' Dr Russell murmured. 'She was scared you would suffer frostbite and lose your toes. Your mother sounds like a resourceful woman.' Dr Russell smiled approvingly.

Her apathy faded for a moment and she wanted to smack the smirk off his face. He was reducing her mother's story to an interesting anecdote in his day.

'Tell me more about your mother,' he asked.

'Long hair.' Azra mimicked her mother's motions in brushing her hair. Those were the moments she cherished from her childhood. How she helped her mother brush her long black hair until it billowed like black silk. 'Work hard,' she continued, her every memory was her mother a whirling dervish of energy as she planted the garden that would guarantee their survival, her back bent under the heavy labour of digging the earth, or rushing from the barn after shovelling manure and milking cows.

'She had a good work ethic,' Dr Russell said. 'Like you.'

He didn't understand. He came from a world where food was found on a shelf, plentiful to all. In her world the only food you had was the one you made yourself. Her mother's hard work was to ensure their survival. What few coins they made her father drank away, but he couldn't do the same with produce.

'Why did you get married when you were so young?' he said. 'You were only seventeen years old.'

She didn't know how to answer the question.

'Did your parents force you?' he prodded.

She wished it were that simple. It was a series of events outside of her control and before she knew it, she was married.

Her husband Mirsad came to Bosnia to find a bride. She was invited to visit friends of the family. She'd heard talk about Mirsad and knew that he would be there, but she was naïve as to what the true nature of this visit entailed. She went, curious to see this strange man from Australia that had the village agog with gossip.

She'd been disappointed by his homespun appearance. He was sturdy in build and even though they were matched in height, he dwarfed her with his robust presence. Working on a tobacco farm under the harsh Australian sun had browned his skin, the lines on his face were deep crevices making him look much older than his twenty-eight years of age.

'Isn't he dark and handsome?' Kadira asked with a smile.

Azra nodded, her eyes on the ground, too embarrassed to look him in the eye. She lagged behind her peers who were already well versed in their physical preferences toward the opposite sex. While the adults spoke she snuck looks at Mirsad and evaluated him. She concluded that he wasn't ugly, but neither was he handsome. He was just an ordinary man, with an ordinary face. He caught her glance and smiled. Except for his eyes, they were doe eyed and full of gentleness.

'Our young buck passes the test.' Kadira laughed heartily when she intercepted the look.

Her cheeks flushed and Azra looked away, her anger a hard ball that sat in her mute mouth. The adults interpreted her gesture as a sign of a modest young woman. Soon after Kadira's husband escorted Mirsad out of the house.

'He's a good man,' Kadira told her as they gathered the dishes.

Azra made her excuses and left as soon as she could. The sun was moving across the sky, marking the day running away from her and she still had many chores to perform. She forgot about the ordinary young man and her strange visit.

The next day she was watching the cows graze at a pasture a few houses from her own. She loved the quiet as she stood outside. There were no shouting voices, no cruel words that bit into her thin flesh, no hard blows that made her tremble and shake, just the gentle sounds of the wind rustling the leaves in the trees, birds tweeting and chirruping, and the soft breeze caressing her bare arms as the sun warmed her inside out.

She tensed as a booming voice called her name, but smiled her relief and waved at Kadira's husband and the young man from Australia.

'We're going to get your father's permission for you to marry Mirsad,' Kadira's husband's voice boomed across the field. 'If you don't want us to continue, speak up now girl.'

She didn't know how to describe the inertia that gripped her as Kadira's husband waited for her answer. Her survival at home depended on her ability to not draw attention to herself during her parents' fights. She learnt to block out everything and disappear within the confines of her imagination. She did the only thing she knew how. She made herself small and invisible. They took her silence as consent and continued on their quest, while she watched the cows, attempting to drift back into the moment of nothingness they had interrupted.

Dr Russell was still waiting for an answer. 'Better life from parents,' she repeated Kadira's explanation for arranging the meeting in the first place.

'Do you remember coming to hospital?' he asked, his eyes searching her face.

A flash of memory burst in her head like a sunbeam. Two nurses were holding her down. She was screaming, 'Help her.

Please help her.' Dr Russell appeared by her side holding a needle that he stabbed into her arm.

Azra jerkily shook her head, her palms sweating with anxiety.

'Our time is up.' Dr Russell closed his clipboard. 'I feel we're making real progress.' He gave a self-satisfied smile as he stretched.

Azra left his office and returned to the room she shared with three other women. She was in time for her medication. The nurse administering the tablets waited while she swallowed before moving to the next bed.

'Vivian, open,' the nurse demanded after the patient swallowed.

Vivian was a new patient and had been cheeking her meds, hiding the tablets in her cheek to be disposed of later. Vivian shook her head, her mouth firmly closed for the first time since she was admitted the day before.

Vivian was diagnosed as Manic Depressive and was still on a high. She jerked like a small bird, her body moving in imperceptible twitches while the words spat out of her mouth like the unending molten lava spewing from an exploding volcano.

Vivian came to hospital when her parents became concerned with her unusual vivacity. Her friends dropped off, exhausted by her loquaciousness and grandiose plans, and her fiancé called off their wedding a week before it was to take place.

'Open your mouth or I'll call another nurse and we'll force-feed you,' the nurse threatened.

After a moment of resistance Vivian opened her mouth sullenly.

'Why can't you be a good girl like Azra,' the nurse said.

Vivian poked her tongue out obscenely. The nurse wrinkled her nose in disgust before moving on to the bed opposite Vivian's.

Thoula was the polar opposite of Vivian. She had four children and in the hustle and bustle of mothering no one realised she hadn't spoken in six months. It was only when her housework became lax and she stopped getting out of bed that they sought help. They called their priest who used holy water to purge her of devils. The purging didn't work and she continued lying in bed. When she didn't eat for five days they called a doctor. She came to hospital emaciated and dull eyed.

Vivian caught Azra staring. 'Fucking dago,' she muttered.

Azra turned her head and stared at the wall opposite. Vivian was full of hatred for the hospital and its demand for conformity. She fought each battle as if it was a matter of life and death. In a way it was. The hospital was premised on the theory that the patient was malfunctioning. Through the rigorous efforts of the doctors in dissembling their brains, they would then be reprogrammed and deemed fit to re-enter society.

Azra felt that each act of complicity stole a piece of her soul, but years of her father's tyranny had programmed her to comply. She was sad Vivian's recalcitrance would end.

Silence descended as two nurses wheeled a gurney into the room. On it lay Cheryl, the only indication she was still alive was the faint rise of her chest. The nurses placed her onto the bed, her head flopped and her limbs flayed.

'What's wrong with her?' Vivian demanded loudly.

No one answered.

'I'm not going to end up like her?' Vivian asked suspiciously.

'Of course not,' the nurse lied as they left.

Cheryl was diagnosed Schizophrenic like Azra. She maintained that God talked to her and she had to follow his orders. She came to hospital after God told her to purify her husband with fire and she set their bed alight. He woke when his leg caught fire and escaped with only a burn mark on his thigh.

Vivian's family came to visit, a troupe of concerned family members who gathered around her bed and listened to her with bemused expressions. Azra surreptitiously took her cigarettes from under her pillow and left the room.

Azra walked out of the front doors. The hospital was on large grounds. For a moment she was disoriented. The way the bright sun lit up the green grass reminded her of home. She expected to see her favourite cow Brena grazing, her white tail swatting the flies away.

Brena loved strawberries and had an unerring knack for finding them in the pasture. Azra used to follow her around, smacking her away from the bushes before Brena scooped them up with her snout. She closed her eyes and tasted the tartness on her tongue.

Someone pushed into her as they walked past and she opened her eyes. The green grass didn't look anything like home. There was a faint yellow tinge where the sun had leeched the colour. Azra forced herself to keep walking. This happened a thousand times a day. She'd experience a moment of déjà vu and retreat back to her homeland in her mind.

She shivered. The chill of evening made her skin break out in goosepimples. As she watched the sun disappear behind the horizon dread seeped into her lungs making it difficult to breathe. She'd learnt to hate the nights. Eventually the cold outside forced her back inside. After a lukewarm dinner of meat swimming in gravy and three veg, it was lights out.

The door was open, the sliver of light from the corridor forming a triangle on the ceiling. The muffled sounds of the night nurses chatting carried down the corridor and into the room.

Vivian twitched and moaned in her bed. Even in sleep she gained no respite from her affliction. Cheryl snored robustly, her tight sinuses making her each breath sound like a pig grunting as it foraged for food. Thoula sniffled quietly, crying in her sleep, her mouth soundlessly forming one word over and over, Mama.

Azra stared at the ceiling, her hands scrunching the sheets against her chest, as she fought the heavy blanket of sleep. Every night she fought the battle and every night she lost, the medication dragging her deep into unconsciousness, making her head spin as she closed her eyes, and there was only the sound of static in her ears, her breathing evened out and she was under the spell of the Sandman.

Her eyes rolled behind her closed eyelids, and her fingers twitched, as she fought a spectre in her dreams, but she could not break through the spell and wake up. In her dream she was falling down a deep vortex, her hands reaching for a hold, until she landed with a thud on the ground. She lifted herself on her elbows, a heavy mass pushing against her stomach. She looked down and saw her stomach was heavy and distended, pressing into the dirt. Something writhed against her skin. She cupped her round stomach and felt movement against her hand.

She heard a high-pitched scream as someone called her name, begging for help. She stood, but now she was in a puddle of blood. The puddle became a pond and her feet were sinking. She tried to scream, but no sound came out. She lurched forward, the blood making a sucking noise as she fought the mud to release her foot. She ran, her gait slow and shuffling, panting as foliage crackled and broke behind her, as if someone was chasing her.

'Good morning, sleepy head,' a bright voice called out.

Azra opened her eyes, the bright sunshine made her squint.

'Time for your treatment,' the nurse said.

She smelt the food as it was served to the other patients and her stomach rumbled.

'Someone hurt.' Azra fought to remember the images of her dream.

'Of course, dear,' the nurse said as she led her to the treatment room.

'Need help.' Azra tried to pull away from her. 'Someone need help.'

The nurse lay her down on the bed. 'We'll talk after your treatment.' She rubbed anaesthetic on Azra's temples. The familiar nausea rose in her empty stomach.

'Bite down,' the nurse said as she thrust a rubber plug in Azra's mouth.

Azra tried to remember every image from her dream. Dread built inside her. She had to stop him hurting her. She had to stop him. An electric volt burst into her brain. Her thoughts disintegrated into nothingness and her body spasmed. White static filled her head.

She woke up in her own bed, the sun had moved past her window, it was late morning. The hunger in her stomach was ripping her apart. She waited for the food tray. There was a flittering thought like she was forgetting something, in the next moment it was gone like the annoying buzz of a mosquito as it flies by. She watched the clock and waited for lunchtime.

Fragments

I threw open the front door and bolted out of the house when my mother's guttural scream of terror stopped me dead in my tracks.

I turned and went back inside. 'What's wrong?'

Mama clutched the wall, her face white with terror. 'Stupid girl!' She shook me by my shoulders. 'You can't run out like that! Snipers will get you.'

Like a long thin finger, my hometown of Srebrenica stretched in the valley between steep hills, clustered along the main road leading in and out of town. The green canopy of the birch tree forest looked like green fairy floss dotted with the burgundy terracotta tile roofs of white rendered houses. The nearby hills were a perfect vantage point for snipers. In the time it took them to shoot once, miss, and correct their target, an innocent bystander would have time to take just one step.

'She'll be fine out the door; it's halfway down the street that they can sight you,' my brother Emir said.

I smiled at him. I was excited to leave the house. In the three months since the war started I hadn't been allowed to leave. My brother and father went to the black market together to buy us what food they could, while I remained home to keep me safe. My parents kept telling me that soon the war would be over and then I'd be able to go where I wanted. Now they had finally accepted there was no end in sight and I couldn't remain a prisoner in my own house 24 hours a day. I was allowed to accompany Mama and my brother to town to make a phone call.

Mama took my hand and stepped out of the house, her eyes fearfully scanning the hills around us as if she could spot the sniper with her naked eye. Her hand clenched mine tightly. We walked down the streets of Srebrenica and it was like I was seeing a new world. There were plastic sheets covering holes in roofs and windows, and parts of houses missing sections. I turned to look at our house as we walked away. My father had been repairing our house between shelling, determined not to let the enemy win in their campaign to wear us down. Even though two of our windows were covered with plastic sheets after the glass had shattered during shelling, and my bedroom window was boarded up as it faced the mountains, it still looked better than most of the houses on our street.

As we walked closer to town, the buildings were more damaged. There were large craters on the sidewalk where *krmače*, the homemade bombs filled with metal and nails that were dropped from aeroplanes had left behind. There were large holes in buildings and some were almost reduced to rubble. My excitement at being out of the house was fading and terror filled me. The streets I used to skip down were now filled with craters.

'The Četniks purposely target the centre of town so we can admire their might.' Emir held out his hand to encompass the destruction around us, using the slur we used against the Serbs. 'They're bullies and we won't let them win.'

I nodded and straightened my shoulders. Fuck the Četniks. I wasn't going to let them make me afraid. Before the war most of the people on the street were the familiar faces of my neighbours. Now I mostly saw strangers. Since the villages around town had been cleared by Četniks, refugees had flooded the town. They were living in school buildings, former houses and flats that belonged to Serbs who had escaped. You could tell the refugees as they were mostly peasants from the villages, the women were in *dimije* – harem-type pants – worn mostly by women in villages, and the men wore French berets.

Those of us from Srebrenica who had access to our own wardrobes wore our best finery when we dared leave our homes. I was wearing my pink and white polka dot summer dress. I had grown and it was feeling tight around the chest and was above my knees, but Mama declared it was still decent.

We walked to the small yellow building in the centre of the town; its huge aerial sticking out on the roof made it the only source of communication with the outside world. The long queue stretched down the street. Mama was calling my uncle who lived in Australia. She would wait for up to three hours to only spend five minutes allocated by the man who operated the rickety army-green radio set – a ham radio – a relic in the time of telephones. A saviour in war.

'We're going to the playground,' I lied to Mama.

'No, wait here with me.' Mama's voice was sharp. She looked at the mountains that girded our small town with suspicion. I followed her gaze and felt goose pimples rise on my skin. I could almost feel the malevolence of the Četniks spying on us from the hills, ready to shoot mothers and children.

'It's okay, I'll be with her,' Emir said.

I drew strength from his calm demeanour. 'Please, Mama, we just want to play. We'll be around the corner.'

Mama bit her lip. 'All right.' She exhaled. 'But only for half an hour.'

'Thank you, Mama.' I hugged her. Her arms grasped me tightly, like she wouldn't let me go. I pulled away and her grasp loosened. Emir stayed out of range. He considered himself too old for our mother's embrace.

We ran down the street. 'Look here.' Emir pointed at the concrete school playground as we walked past where the hopscotch chalk marks now framed a crater. 'A woman and child were hit by bombs dropped from two Yugoslav fighter aeroplanes. They had to scrape what was left of them with a shovel.' He peered closer trying to see fragments of flesh and bone.

'That's gross,' I said, and sped up.

'Why? It's what happens during war.'

I turned to see Emir's face. He was matter-of-fact, untouched by emotion as he spoke about the woman. I sped away, veering right only to abruptly stop, my eyes taking in the destroyed school. The day before a 'mosquito' had flown into the city and dropped its destructive load. The mosquito had circled the town for half an hour, looking for blood. Usually the improvised bombs, or boilers as we called them, fell onto the slopes, causing a tremendous crash and leaving a crater behind. But yesterday the bomb had landed onto the school. The two-storey school was now a mess of rubble. The bomb had split it in two. All the windows were shattered and the gaping holes reminded me of a screaming monster in a horror movie.

'Were they trying to hit the school?' I asked.

'They were probably hoping there were students inside.'

I didn't want to believe that people could be so evil and want to kill children. 'Maybe the pilot was trying to hit the town and miscalculated?'

'Don't be naive. They don't care if their targets are children or not. The only good *Balija* is a dead *Balija*,' he said using the slur that our enemy called us. To them we were descendants of the Turkish Ottoman Empire, infidels that they had to clear out.

Now as we wrestled with our courage to enter the school, I peered up at the sky fearfully. I hated the mosquitos the most – even more than the jet planes that broke the sound barrier, wreaking their destruction before they disappeared. The high-pitched sound of mosquitoes was imprinted into my brain. At times like this when the sky was bright blue and clear of any aeroplanes, the whine echoed in my head so I couldn't be sure if the noise was a figment of my imagination or a warning of real danger.

'We'd better get this done,' Emir said.

I nodded.

Since we had repelled the attacks, life had become a series of monotonous segments of starvation and boredom, broken only by shelling from the Četniks on the hills surrounding us. They controlled the borders and there was no food aid coming in or out. I had become used to the cramps in my stomach, but my mind hungered for a respite from my life. My only escape were the pages of a book, and the only books were from the school library.

Before the bombing Emir and his friends regularly raided the library and exchanged books and I was the recipient of his largesse, but I was bored reading his books. It was time for me take part and find my own, however, now that I was standing in front of my former school all I could think about was my life before the war. I wanted to scream at the stupid girl I used to be who had spent hours counting down the minutes until the end of the school day.

I carefully pulled myself through the broken window and stepped over shards of glass, listening to the sky, barely breathing at every rustle. I crept through the broken corridors and passed by the classroom that I'd started grade four in, before the war, before the darkness invaded my world. My best friend Zora and I sat in the back row together on a desk that was now scarred from shelling. Sometimes we'd whisper under our breath, but we had to be careful or our teacher Mrs Tanović punished us. Most of the time we passed notes to each other, starting with a sheet of paper that we filled by the end of the day. Sometimes I'd read over the sheets I kept, remembering the days when my life was full of mundane details like complaints about Teacher's Pet Tereza, the boredom of reciting the times table, and rolling my eyes as my peers butchered *Anne of Green Gables* with their stilted reading.

Emir stopped beside me. 'Bad memories?'

'I wonder where Zora is and what she's thinking,' I said, my eyes burning.

'She's on the other side. Probably wants us dead.'

'She's my friend. I don't believe that.'

Emir opened his mouth like he wanted to say something, but he paused. 'She *was* your friend,' he finally said.

I rubbed my throbbing chest. I had imagined that one day things would be normal again. Zora would come back to live next door and we would play in the forest behind our houses like we'd done our whole lives. But this was my new normal.

We reached the library. Part of the wall had collapsed, and the ceiling had caved in. Some of the books had been exposed to the elements and were pulpy from the dew and useless, but there was a corner where they had been protected. I crept to the corner, collecting books as I went. We peered up at the sky through a crack in the ceiling, hearing the whine of the mosquito plane approaching.

'Come back!' Emir demanded.

But I wasn't going to be deterred. Who knew when I could come back, or if there would be anything to come back to? Emir grabbed my arm, and we ran back to the window. As we stepped over the windowsill I dropped my books and bent to pick them up. 'Leave them,' Emir shouted and tugged my arm, making me run as the engine whine got closer.

I paused, gasping for breath near the playground, above the red stain on the concrete. I peered closer, seeing a bone fragment on the ground that the shovel had missed.

Nervous Breakdowns

I entered the bedroom where my mum was still lying in bed. I had poured myself cereal, then found there was no milk.

'Oh,' Mum said when I told her. She sat up in bed with her hair tousled, blinking sleep out of her green eyes. Izet, my new stepfather, had left to run errands an hour ago and we were alone. 'Take some money from my purse and go buy it.'

I bit back words of frustration. I missed Nana. During the four years that I had lived with my grandparents in Bosnia, in the mornings she would wake me and I'd find breakfast waiting for me on the table: hot tea, sliced homemade bread, jar of also homemade jam and a stick of butter. In the two weeks I'd been living with Mum again I'd learnt that I had to fend for myself. Mum suffered from what she called *Slom Živaca*, which translated to 'nervous breakdowns' in English, and all my childhood she had been in and out of hospital. Living with my grandparents had been a welcome reprieve from the chaos of Mum's illness, even though at the same time I'd been wracked with a feeling of homesickness and grief at being separated from her.

As I rode my bicycle to the milk bar, I enjoyed the sensation of flying. My mood lightened. I looked with curiosity at the yellow and brown brick houses I passed. These were the same streets I'd walked as a young child, but now as a twelve year old it was as if I was seeing them with the eyes of a stranger. This landscape was so different from Bosanska Gradiška, the town where my grandparents lived. By comparison Melbourne's western suburbs were monochrome and cold. There was concrete everywhere: in grey footpaths and asphalt roads, and most of the yards were lost to concrete driveways.

On my way back home, the plastic bag with the milk bottle hanging on my handlebar kept swinging back and forth, until its handle tore. The bottle hit the asphalt with a bang, the milk seeping into the black bitumen. I braked abruptly and stared at the mess on the road. I didn't know what to do. I had no money to buy another bottle, as I'd taken only a two-dollar coin from my mother's purse. I began peddling toward home.

Fear gripped me the closer I got. I didn't know what Mum would do. If this had happened while I was living in Bosnia, my grandfather would have used a stick to correct my clumsiness. His favourite method of punishment was beating my fingertips while I held them together. As for my grandmother, she would have chased me away from home, throwing rocks at my retreating form. Even though I thought she purposely missed with her rock throwing, no one could be that bad, but I'd never stuck around to test my theory.

When I arrived home, I knocked on the door, as I wanted the option of a quick get-away if Mum got agro. I had never before feared my mother, but I had become infected with fear after living in a Communist regime where people who were different from the so-called 'norm' were viewed as dangerous and often locked in institutions. While we lived in Bosnia Mum, too, was incarcerated in hospital whenever she demonstrated the tiniest indication of her illness.

'Why are you knocking?' Mum asked when she opened the door.

'The milk bottle smashed and it went everywhere on the road,' I was almost in tears.

Mum sighed, her lips narrowing in displeasure. 'Here.' She handed me a coin.

'Thanks.'

I walked back to my bike, worrying my lip. Maybe living with Mum was going to be better than living with my grandparents.

Six months later I was hanging out on the corner of my street with other neighbourhood kids. Even though it was seven o'clock at night, it was summer, the sun was still out and it was broad daylight. I was with Zehra, the daughter of Mum's best friend. Zehra had recently moved into a shared house not far from where we lived.

The squeal of a burnout rent the air, the thick vapour produced by the friction of tyres on asphalt surrounding the car like a blanket of smoke. Zehra stood on the curb wearing denim cut offs and a stretchy spaghetti top that was poured onto her hourglass figure, her nipples beaded from the cold.

The red Holden Commodore passed by and Zehra stared dead ahead at the driver who was speeding past us. I saw the moment when she caught his eye, how his head whipped toward her and their stares locked, then he drove past. Another squeal of the tyres and he did a U-turn, before pulling to a stop by us.

The driver was speaking to one of the guys who we were hanging with while staring at Zehra. She kept looking down at the ground, then quickly back up at him. With each drop of her eyes she did a move, drawing attention to yet another asset of hers: a dip of her shoe in the street curb to show off her naked leg, a scratch of her shoulder which squeezed her unfettered boobs up. By lowering her eyes. she gave the guy a chance to check her out, then met his gaze again.

I was both fascinated and appalled. At thirteen, I'd just begun developing and my breasts were the size of apricots.

'I'd better go get ready,' Zehra said and broke away from the group. It was Friday night and she was going clubbing. She was five years older than me and her world was full of freedom: she didn't have to deal with parental dramas and decided herself where she lived and with whom, while my life was always dictated by Mum's illness.

Having no interest in hanging around with hoodlums once Zehra was out of the picture, I went back home. Mum was in hospital again and without her my stepfather and I had settled into a loose routine. We lived off frozen pizzas, baked beans and hot dogs. Before Mum married my stepfather, whenever she went to hospital, life as I knew it would stop. I would be taken in by friends of family or foster families, would have to change schools and leave my friends behind, and I would be in limbo because there was no time limit as to how long Mum's hospital stay would last. At least now I got to go to the same school, hang out with my friends, stay in the same house. Still, I avoided home as much as possible, staying out late on school nights. I found spending time with Izet draining.

Izet was caught up in homesickness. While living in Bosnia he had worked as a baker and had lived with his elderly parents and brother. Now that he had left, the memories of his previous life were coloured by nostalgia, which rendered it as perfect. By contrast Australia was found wanting. According to Izet, there was no proper sense of community here, and he felt an all pervasive sense of violence outside his front door. Indeed, the western suburbs of Melbourne where we then lived were often described as the crime capital and our suburb, St Albans, had the highest murder rates in Victoria. In his unhappiness, Izet became consumed with talking about leaving this 'shit country', though he never did anything about it. But even though being in Izet's company made me feel anxious and unsettled, I couldn't ignore the fact that without him in the picture I would once again be at the mercy of strangers to care for me while Mum was in hospital. Mum's previous beaus had been off-hand in accepting her offspring, while Izet cared for me as if I was his biological daughter, even though I kept him at a distance because I never trusted that he would stick around.

The next morning I woke up with my head throbbing, and my back and pelvis muscles aching. I lolled on the couch trying to watch *Rage*, feeling uncomfortable. During a commercial break I went to the toilet and saw blood on my underwear. I had only found out about periods when I started high school, from my girlfriends. My grandparents had kept me sheltered while I lived with them. Even though I knew what a period was, I'd somehow never realised that I would be afflicted by it.

I stuffed toilet paper into my underwear, then yanked the phone into my bedroom, stretching the cord to its limit, and closed the door. The phone rang out once. 'Oh, God, please be home,' I begged as I dialed again.

'What?' Zehra's voice finally came on. She sounded half asleep and belligerent.

'It's Alma,' I whispered.

'Who?'

I repeated my name again, louder.

'Why are you calling so early?' Zehra moaned.

'I got my period,' I whispered, aware of my stepfather in the living room.

'So? Hang on, is this your first period?'

'Yes,' I said. 'I don't know what to do. Mum is in hospital and I can't talk to Izet.'

'Didn't your mum buy you pads?'

'No.' My tears gathered. 'I put in some toilet paper, but I don't know how long it's going to work.'

'Okay, I'm coming over.'

I hung up the phone and waited at the front of the house. A few minutes later I saw the red Holden Commodore pull up and Zehra came out.

'Here, take these.' She handed me a plastic bag with pads. 'This should last you a couple of days and if you need any more you can call me. Make sure you change them frequently.'

Burn Out Guy from the night before beeped the horn.

'Gotta go. I'll come by tomorrow. We'll talk then.' Zehra waved as she got into the car.

Burn Out Guy did another screeching burnout as they disappeared back around the corner. I returned home, put a pad between my legs and went to bed. The throbbing in my back had increased and now cramping in my abdomen had also started. When I woke, Mum was home for a weekend stay, eating breakfast in the kitchen. The medication was flattening her mood and I could see she was lethargic, struggling to maintain energy.

'You're being lazy today,' she snapped as soon as she noticed me. 'The least you can do is wash the dishes.' She pointed at the full sink.

I avoided housework at the best of times and this didn't change while Mum was in hospital. Izet picked up the slack, but still there would be a bit of housework waiting for Mum whenever she was home for the weekend.

Now at least I had a genuine reason for my slackness. I felt heavy and defeated by the force of what was happening to my body, and worn down by pain. 'I got my period,' I whispered.

'Oh.' Mum went silent for a moment. 'Do you need pads?'

'No, I got some from Zehra,' I enjoyed seeing the consternation on her face. She had failed to prepare me for this rite of passage. 'I need you to buy more.'

'I'll tell Izet to add it to his list,' Mum said. My stepfather was the one who did the grocery shopping.

'What? No I don't want him to buy them for me.'

Mum didn't say anything.

'Just give me money and I'll do it myself.'

She handed me a note.

'Hey, put that back, *mala*,' my stepdad said, using his nickname for me—little one—as I snatched the remote and changed the channel.

'*Booker* is about to start.'

At fifteen, I was boy-crazy and had spent the afternoon in feverish anticipation for my favourite TV show. It was a spin-off from *21 Jump Street*, an incredibly unrealistic show that featured young gorgeous police officers going undercover in high schools. *Booker* had Richard Grieco, the object of my latest crush. I had his posters on my wall with lipstick marks all over them and had even sent a letter to his fan club, receiving a signed photo for my efforts.

'I was watching that doco,' Izet said.

I ignored him, keeping my back to him. We had one TV and it was a constant source of battles between Izet and me with Mum hardly getting a look in.

Izet took back the remote control and switched the channel.

'Put it back,' I yelled. 'It's about to start!'

'Alma,' Mum said. 'It's Izet's turn to watch.'

'But it's *Booker*...'

'You can't always get to watch what you want,' Mum said, calmly. 'You have to share. You watched *Quantum Leap* yesterday and Izet didn't watch his show.'

'You always take his side!' I shouted. 'You know I love this TV show and I watch it every week. He shouldn't be watching this crap anyway.'

Usually at this point my stepdad would crumble and tell Mum to let it go, but not this time. Maybe he'd had enough. I had been hogging the TV. I had my roster of television shows I was completely incapable of giving up.

'I told you it's his turn.' Mum changed the channel.

I got up and switched the channel again using the buttons below the screen, then sat back down. The theme song *Hot in the City* sung by Billy Idol was playing and I felt the familiar wave of excitement at seeing my crush on the big screen. I swayed to the beat, literally rubbing my hands.

The channel changed again.

'What the fuck did you do that for!' I yelled. 'I fucking told you I was watching that!' I continued ranting, uttering all sorts of profanity, while Izet adopted his usual turtle pose, hunching into himself as if he was trying to protect himself from my words. He was a mild-mannered man who always, anxiously, retreated in the face of my adolescent rage.

'Alma, enough,' Mum said. 'Go to your room.'

'No!' I stood in front of the television so Izet couldn't watch. This battle, for me, was more than a battle over the television. I was really fighting for Mum's attention.

I had never forgiven her for marrying Izet and leaving me in Bosnia while they came to Australia as newlyweds. Mum and I had gone to Bosnia for a visit that stretched out to a four year stay. The medication in Bosnia didn't manage to control Mum's symptoms and her parents kept hospitalising her every six months. She couldn't bear this any longer and after marrying Izet her plan had been that we all return to Australia together, but I refused. Fearing the chaos that I'd lived through when Mum was a single parent, unsure things would be any different even after her marriage, I had chosen to stay with my grandparents. Even though Mum returned to Bosnia a year later for me and we finally returned to Australia together, I wanted her to prove to me that I was her number one. Her siding with Izet made me think she loved him more. The rejection fuelled my rage.

'Go to your room or I'm going to get the *oklagija*,' Mum said, threatening to hit me with a long rolling pin that resembled a broom handle and was used to make pita.

I switched the channel and sat back down in front of the TV. When I was a child Mum would use a wooden spoon after three warnings, but she had phased that out when I was a pre-teen. Even though I doubted that she would hit me, I'd never been willing to test her and usually the threat alone would be enough for me to mend my ways, but on this night my lust for Richard Grieco overpowered my fear.

Mum hit me lightly on the head from behind with the *oklagija*. It was more like a tap, but that didn't matter to me.

'You fucking hit me!' I shouted, crying. 'How dare you hit me?'

I ran to my bedroom, slamming the door and crying furiously, messily. I felt rejected. The pain of that was ripping through me, the same pain I had felt while I missed her in Bosnia. She didn't love me. She had never loved me and what happened now proved it.

Mum knocked on the door: 'Come back. We've changed the channel. You can watch your show.'

I wavered for a moment. Of course I wanted to perve on Richard Grieco, but I wasn't going to give her the satisfaction. She hit me. She was going to pay for this.

'No, I don't want anything to do with you!' I shouted. 'I fucking hate you both.'

I heard Mum's footsteps retreat. I opened my window and jumped out. I wheeled my bicycle from the backyard and rode the five kilometres to Zehra's place. She had moved out of the share house and was living by herself in a bungalow behind a house in Sunshine.

There were no lights and when I knocked on the door she didn't answer. I didn't want to go home and settled on her front step to wait. An hour passed and I was flagging. Then I heard a car pull up at the front of the house. Zehra appeared through the side gate accompanied by a man. They stopped to kiss, while I shuffled my feet in embarrassment, not sure whether I should interrupt or not.

The boy saw me and pushed Zehra away. She looked at me over her shoulder: 'What are you doing here?'

'I ran away from home. Mum hit me on the head.' I was crying again.

She hesitated. 'I guess you'd better come in then.' She unlocked the door. 'This is Milan.' She introduced me as her friend and I felt a glow.

'We've got to call your mum,' Zehra said. She had no phone installed in her flat so she took me to the phone box around the corner.

I didn't want to call Mum. I wanted her, and my stepfather too, to suffer, but Zehra told me if Mum called the police to look for me she would get in trouble. Mum agreed to let me stay the night and said they would come by tomorrow to pick me up.

Back at Zehra's I sat across from Milan, checking out his biceps peeking from his t-shirt, while Zehra made coffee. 'So what happened?' she asked, blowing the steam on her mug.

I told her. 'I hate her and I hate living there,' I muttered, picking at the laminate on the side of the table. 'I can't wait to get out of there.'

'I know.' Zehra squeezed my hand. 'But you've still got another three years at least.'

I sighed. I felt like I was a prisoner and freedom was too far out of reach.

The next morning Mum came by, her lips tightened in displeasure and anger. She kept her eyes away from me as if I didn't exist.

She and Zehra and my stepdad spoke in the bungalow while I waited outside. When they finished, Izet and Mum left without saying a word to me.

'What happened?' I was feeling deflated. Out of all the reactions I'd expected, this wasn't it.

'Your mum agreed to let you stay here for the weekend. Give everyone a chance to cool down,' Zehra said, as we went back inside.

It was as I suspected. They didn't want me around.

'I'll have to call Milan and tell him I can't go clubbing tonight.'

'Why can't you go?'

'Last time I checked, you're not eighteen.'

'Oh.' I was disappointed that I wouldn't have the fun weekend I had hoped for.

'Maybe there is something we can do. We can ask my friend Jules for her ID.' Zehra looked at me critically and sighed. 'I don't know if it will work.'

'Please, please, can we try?'

The photo on the laminated card looked nothing like me. Jules was an overweight girl with brown eyes and dyed blonde hair, her dark regrowth visible, while I was naturally blonde, blue eyed and thin.

'Don't worry. It will work.' Zehra ruffled my hair. She leant me her clothes. We dressed identically in denim cut offs that had a dangling string, singlet tops with push up bras, frilly socks and high heels. We went to *Hot Gossip*, a nightclub in the industrial estates of Sunshine, which was the den of the western suburbs' try-hards.

The bouncer looked me up and down and asked for ID. I handed over Jules', looking away all the while. The bouncer looked suspiciously at the card, but eventually jerked his head, indicating we could go in. Zehra had predicted this, speculating he would be too scared he'd be made a fool if he challenged me openly, because girls could drastically change their appearance.

Inside, my eyes struggled to adjust to the darkness. Once they did, and I began dancing, I noticed a hot guy on the dance floor. He was tall and lithe, wearing all white. This was the time of MC Hammer and the harem pants, and this guy was a 'would-be-MC.' Our eyes met and I felt a zing. We slowly moved toward each other. His hand was now on my back, my hand on his shoulder. I looked up at him and we locked lips. I don't know how long the kiss lasted, it felt like forever and it felt like a second. There was no awkwardness or bumping of noses I had experienced before. It was so easy, so perfect.

The would-be-MC asked me if I wanted to take a walk. I stared at him, overwhelmed with the whole experience. He repeated the question. Embarrassment overcame me and I ran to the toilet to hide in a cubicle.

Zehra, who thought I'd indeed gone for a 'walk' with the boy, searched for me in the backseats of the cars in the car park. Milan told me later that she'd been crying all the while, saying that she didn't want me to lose my virginity in the back of a car. Eventually someone told Zehra where I was hiding.

She found me in the toilet. I wasn't alone there – a girl with brown bouffant hair was primping herself in the mirror. She'd taken off her bra and only wore a white t-shirt. I just wanted to go home, but, as we were about to leave, the toilet door slammed open and a man burst in. He walked up to the girl, clocked her in the face with his fist, and rushed off in a blur of fury.

Zehra helped the girl up. The force of the blow had knocked her into a cubicle; she'd fallen over the toilet bowl and lay dazed beside it.

'Yeah, yeah, I'm fine.' Bouffant Girl shook her head like she was trying to shake off the dazed feeling. She stood and straightened her shoulders. 'If that cunt thinks I'm not going to go out there, he can fuck himself!'

'Who was he?' I asked.

'My boyfriend.' She strutted out, her jaw already swelling up.

We followed her to a makeshift stage, where she joined the four girls standing on it. 'What's your name?' a cheesy MC asked each one of them, engaging them in small talk before he got a water bottle and sprayed their t-shirts. The cold water plastered the cotton to their breasts and made their nipples bead up. The crowd of rowdy boys cheered. 'Take it off, take it off,' they chanted.

Bouffant Girl smiled a sickly smile and took off the t-shirt, standing on stage bare breasted. We'd seen enough and left.

The next night we went to *Hot Gossip* again. This time the bouncer just waved us through. We were in the toilets when the door burst open. It was Bouffant Girl. There was a dark bruise on her face and murder in her eyes.

'Hey, how are you doing?' Zehra smiled at her.

Bouffant Girl walked past her and up to me. She swung back her fist and sucker punched me in the face. I went down like a ton of bricks.

'What the fuck!' Zehra pushed Bouffant Girl away.

While she bent down to help me up, Bouffant Girl walked out of the toilet, a strut in her hips. Zehra and her mates went looking for Bouffant Girl, but she'd done a runner, knowing that payback would be coming. Later one of Zehra's friends told her that the bouncer had found out my age and hadn't taken kindly to being lied to. He'd wanted me to learn my lesson and not return again so he'd asked Bouffant Girl, who was his friend, to scare me off.

While being punched had been unpleasant, it wasn't a new experience. Growing up in the western suburbs I'd had my head kicked in three times already and regaling my weekend adventures to my schoolmates had transformed me from a forgettable nobody to a cool somebody, but now I was beginning to question whether the price for being Zehra's shadow was too high. Maybe Zehra wasn't as cool as I thought she was?

Back at school on Monday I had an appointment with Miss Beattie, the school counsellor. I had started seeing her a few months before at the principal's request. Mum was having frequent breakdowns, on average every six months, and when she was sick I stayed home to look after her. She couldn't stand my stepfather when she was sick and would try and kick him out by throwing his clothes on the front lawn. And she couldn't be left alone. On her own, she'd get in the car and drive off to the shopping centre, spending money we didn't have, or go visiting friends for hours, unaware of how intrusive and rude she was being by outstaying her welcome and by blurting out her every thought, even if it was insulting to her hosts.

Mum didn't have a good grasp of English and, when I had to care for her, I used to write notes to the teacher to explain my absences and get her to sign. Soon she was better, but I'd had a taste of the good life: being able to sleep in, watch daytime television and have no homework, and didn't want to return to school. I'd write more notes, faking Mum's signature, and spend the day in the library, reading to escape my life.

Eventually the coordinators twigged and I was called into the principal's office. Sitting beside me was my year nine coordinator, Miss McGee.

'We need to talk to you about your school attendance,' the principal began and I gulped. I had clocked up twenty days off.

He pulled out a stack of notes. 'If you see here, this signature looks different to this signature.' He held up a note from the beginning of the year and one at the end. I'd gotten sloppy with forging Mum's signature, my cursive handwriting bleeding into her fake signature.

'My mum is sick a lot,' I said. 'The medication makes her hand shake, and these are from when she's better and her hand isn't shaking.'

The principal and Miss McGee exchanged a look. 'What kind of illness does she have?' he asked.

I told him about Mum's nervous breakdowns and that I had to take care of her.

'Thank you, Alma,' the principal said when I finished. 'We'll call your mother to confirm what you told us.'

I spent the rest of the day in a state of agitation, anxious to get home. 'Has the principal called you?' I asked Mum as I ran into the living room, gasping for breath.

She shook her head.

I told her about being called into the principal's office: 'You have to cover for me. You have to tell them that you signed all the notes.'

Mum's face had tightened as I spoke. I didn't have to explain to her what was at stake. If the school knew that I'd been wagging, we were both in strife. She would be the mentally ill mother who couldn't control her wayward daughter and the school might involve the Department of Human Services. I had been taken away already a few times in my childhood when she was ill and placed with foster carers. Either way, it was in both of our interests to keep scrutiny off us.

Sure enough, Mum backed me up when the principal called, but as a result the school recommended that I begin seeing the school counsellor. I didn't mind. I got to meet Miss Beattie who actually listened to what I had to say and took me seriously. More importantly, I missed a period of schoolwork a week. I tried to time it so that I missed maths, a subject that I struggled in. I usually spent those classes reading, or would transform myself into the class clown, disrupting the lesson.

'What illness does your mum have?' Miss Beattie asked.

This was the first time that we'd gone into this territory. Usually I spent all my time bitching about my friends.

'Mum has nervous breakdowns.'

'But what is the actual name of the illness?'

'What do you mean? That's the name.' That's what Mum and everyone I knew called it, and that's what I'd grown up telling people.

Miss Beattie asked me what happened when Mum got sick. I explained how she got insomnia and couldn't sleep, her glowing eyes and thick tongue, and the way she would share her every thought and feeling. Miss Beattie nodded as I spoke. I also told her about Mum's bizarre behavior in those times. I said that there seemed to be no rhyme or reason to Mum getting sick. Sometimes she got sick when she was taking her medication, sometimes she got sick when she didn't. She got sick when there was lots of stress, and she got sick when there wasn't. But the one thing that was a constant was the complete shock that I felt every time. It seemed like her nervous breakdowns came out of nowhere and would only become obvious when she was too far gone and all we could do was take her to hospital and wait for the doctors to smack it out of her.

Miss Beattie's questions made me think about Mum differently and I went home that night and asked her what her illness was called.

'Nervous breakdown.'

'Yes, but what causes it?'

'The doctors told me that there's a chemical imbalance in my brain.'

When I returned the next time to talk to Miss Beattie, she had a surprise for me.

'I was thinking about your mum and decided to do some research.' She handed me sheets of paper that were photocopied pages from a book. 'Does this sound like your mum's illness?'

I began reading. The information was about manic depression, what we now know as Bipolar. This illness was characterised by emotional highs and lows. When the person was suffering from mania, they would engage in impetuous and reckless behaviour, which I recognised in my mother. When they suffered from depression, they would struggle to get out of bed and become suicidal. This, too, was what happened with my mother.

As I read, I felt a shock thrumming through my system. I didn't know it at the time, but this moment would change my life. For the first time I realised that there was actually a pattern to my mother's illness. That there were early signs I could recognise if I paid attention and I could get her help before she ended up in hospital. For once I felt a sense of hope, that I could have some control over my life.

I brought the information sheet home. 'Mum, do you think you have manic depression?'

Mum looked at me with curiosity. 'Some doctors said I have schizophrenia, some said manic depression.'

'But if you read this, then it's all about you.' She took the photocopied pages from me and read. 'This is what you have, isn't it?'

Mum nodded.

'Why didn't you say? Why did you call it nervous break-down?'

'That's what we called it at home.'

I had spent so long blaming Mum for her illness and all the horrible things that happened because of it. I had judged her and found her wanting as a mother, a wife, a human being. But now I realised that she was as much a victim of her 'nervous breakdowns' as I was.

That weekend Zehra called me to sleep over. 'Sorry, I can't make it,' I told her. We had made plans earlier in the week and I knew she'd be mad at me for breaking them. In the past, I'd have done anything Zehra wanted me to, but now I had other priorities. 'Mum and I are watching a Doris Day marathon together.'

The Choice

I was shovelling caked manure with a pitchfork into the wheel-barrow, while my older sister Senada cleaned the cow's trough, when she shushed me. I tiptoed toward her and we eaves-dropped. Edin and his friend were outside the barn door speaking in a whisper and we could barely hear them.

'Party?' I whispered.

Senada nodded jerkily, her finger on her lips. She stepped out of the barn after Edin's friend left. 'What party are you going to tonight?' she asked our brother.

'There's no party,' Edin sped up.

'That's not what you said to your friend,' she said.

'You don't know what you heard,' Edin replied.

'What about Babo?' Senada asked.

He stopped in his tracks. Our father was a devout Muslim and did not approve of Edin's social life. In the past few months he'd fallen in with a bad crowd and would be gone all night and come home rumpled and drunk, barely able to do his chores the following day. Our father gave him a sound beating last time he'd gone carousing and had forbidden him from drinking alcohol. If Senada tattled about the party he would be forbidden from going anywhere that night.

'If you take Jasmina and me to the party Babo doesn't need to know anything,' she said.

Edin turned and approached her. 'It's not that kind of a party.' He gripped Senada's arm tightly.

'You're lying. If we don't go, you don't go.' She wrenched her arm out of his grasp.

'Fine.' He threw his hands up. 'You can come.'

Senada smiled coquettishly and twirled her skirt. 'Thank you, Edin.'

He shook his fist as he walked away. Senada blew him a kiss and ran back to me. We giggled as we ran into the house, planning what we would wear to the party.

Even though things were changing in post-World War II Yugoslavia, nothing much had changed in our little backward village. While women in the city had jobs and some freedom, here our brothers could come and go as they pleased, but we girls always missed out.

To guarantee our chastity and keep our reputations safe Babo kept us close to home and our brothers never wanted to chaperone us, but now, thanks to Senada's quick thinking, we were finally going to have a night out.

We snuck out of the window at 9 o'clock that night when everyone was fast asleep. We covered our dresses with work clothes when we left, just in case we were caught, and stripped off when we had walked a few houses away from ours, hiding them in our neighbour's hedge.

Senada got out the red lipstick she'd bought from a pedlar and that she kept hidden in a loose brick in our room. I carefully rubbed some lipstick on her lips.

'Wait up, Edin,' Senada said.

He didn't slow down.

'Where is the party?' she asked him.

Edin hunched his shoulders and increased his pace. I rubbed lipstick on my finger and put it on my lips as we walked. Senada and I exchanged looks and struggled to match his pace, our pretty shoes not well suited to the unsealed road.

We meandered through back streets and across fields for over an hour, our path illuminated by the moon shining above us. The houses got further and further apart the deeper we pressed into the countryside.

By the time we arrived at the party Senada and I were bedraggled, the hair we'd carefully styled before we left was stringy and damp with sweat. Edin turned down a driveway of a farmhouse. I expected he would head to the large home, instead he bypassed the barn, the shed where wood was stored, the stables and chook pen, and headed to the garage where the tractor was parked.

He walked behind the garage and there was a window with light seeping around the curtain edges and a closed door. Senada and I stopped to tidy ourselves, but when Edin disappeared through the door we rushed after him. I'd expected music, talking and laughter. Instead we were in a tiny room with a stove, a threadbare couch, single bed, and a table where five young men sat playing a card game and drinking.

Edin looked at us with a smirk on his face, while the young men watched us suspiciously. I flushed with embarrassment and inched toward the door.

Senada yanked me to a stop by grabbing my arm. She straightened and smiled. 'We heard there was a party here,' she said as she walked into the room. 'Where's the music.' As she made eye contact with the men they thawed and smiled back.

'We didn't know we would have such lovely company,' a young man said as he reached for Senada's hand. 'I'm Karim and this is my little home away from home.'

Senada introduced us. 'We're Edin's sisters.' She looked at Edin who had joined the card game with challenge in her eyes.

'I didn't know you had such lovely sisters,' Karim said loudly to Edin as he handed us each a shot glass of *rakija*, a homemade brew made of fermented plums.

Edin didn't look up from his cards. Karim gave us a rueful smile and led us to the couch. 'Nermin.' Karim waved at a young man across the room.

Nermin lived near us and we knew each other by sight. Our little hamlet numbered thirty houses of families who lived off the harvest we reaped from the land. Our father had the largest parcel that was slowly dwindling as he sold plots to set up older siblings as they married.

Nermin's family was poor and he'd left the village a few years ago and moved to a nearby town to work in a factory so he could support them. His father was a drunkard who'd frittered away all he earnt, leaving his family to struggle. They lived in a ramshackle and tiny one bedroom house, shared by his parents, Nermin and his brother.

Senada took a sip of *rakija* and waved a hand in front of her mouth. 'Try it Jasmina,' she encouraged me, taking another big gulp.

I sipped, my face scrunching up as it dried my mouth. My eyes teared and I nearly choked. Everyone laughed, including Senada. I flushed in embarrassment.

Senada put her hand across my shoulders. 'It gets better the more you drink.'

As the hours passed I sat stiffly, holding the full glass and pretending to sip every few minutes. I didn't want them to laugh at me again.

'Are either of you lovely ladies spoken for?' Karim asked.

Senada shook her head.

Karim put his arm over Nermin's shoulders. 'Because my friend here is looking for a wife.' Nermin looked right at me.

'Oohhh, looks like you have an admirer.' Senada nudged me with her elbow.

I nudged her back, trying to get her to shut up.

'Don't you think my friend is handsome?' Karim patted Nermin's cheeks.

'Oooh, isn't he handsome?' Senada hit me again.

'No, he's not.' I slammed my elbow into her ribs.

She gasped and held her side. 'I was joking.'

Nermin's face flushed and he returned to the card game. Karim gave me a hard look and shook his head. 'That wasn't nice, little girl.'

I stared back at him defiantly. Senada leaned in and whispered something to Karim. They both looked at me and laughed. I looked away. Edin was still playing cards, but he looked worse for the wear. His face was flushed and he weaved drunkenly on his chair.

After an hour of sitting in boredom while everyone else laughed around me I tugged on Senada's arm. 'Let's go home.'

'Why?' Senada almost screamed. 'Aren't you having fun?'

She took hold of my glass and held it to my mouth. It hit my teeth and I jerked back. The *rakija* spilt on my dress.

Senada laughed and took the glass off me, finishing the last few drops. 'That's how you do it.'

Karim's eyes were on my chest. I looked down. The *rakija* had wet the front of my dress and outlined my breasts in stark detail. I covered myself with my hands and bit my lip as tears came to my eyes.

'Don't cry,' Senada said drunkenly. I headed for the door. 'Hold up,' Senada called out.

I looked behind me. She'd stood, but Karim tugged on her arm and said something to her. She flopped back onto the sofa with a laugh.

I walked out the door and to the back of the house where there was a path leading to the outside lavatory. The water pump was next to the barn with a trough beside it. I pumped water into the trough and washed the front of my dress. The smell of *rakija* remained on my skin.

It was a beautiful summer night. The quiet stillness was soothing after the frantic hilarity. I sat on the bench, waiting for my dress to dry before returning to the party, but I must have fallen asleep. When I returned Senada was lying on the couch, her dress lifted revealing her underwear. Karim was standing above her with his hands on his belt buckle.

'What are you doing?' I shouted as I rushed at him.

He moved away from Senada nonchalantly and sat at the table again, lighting up a cigarette. Nermin sat across from him, bent forward with his head on his folded arms.

I yanked down Senada's dress and shook her leg. 'Wake up,' I shouted, but my words didn't penetrate her drunken sleep. 'Where's Edin?' I demanded, realising I wasn't going to be able to get her home by myself.

'Your brother left a long time ago,' Karim said. 'He didn't want the two of you to miss out on the party.'

I kept shaking Senada, but she was like a rag doll.

'I want to go home,' I said, tears in my eyes.

'What's your hurry?' Karim asked. 'We still haven't danced.'

I looked at Nermin, but his eyes were closed and he seemed unaware of what was going on.

Karim stood and pulled me to him. Nermin lifted his head and squinted at us. 'Come on,' Karim pulled him up. 'Dance with the princess.' He threw me at Nermin.

I caught myself from falling by holding onto Nermin's shoulders. My body was pressed against him. His eyes widened and his drowsy face cleared.

'Let go.' I pushed him and he fell back onto his chair. I ran to the door.

Karim came after me and pulled me to a stop. As we struggled his hand caught on the front of my dress and he ripped it. The cool air brushed against my bare breast and my nipple hardened.

Karim licked his lips. I tried to pull away, but he held me against him. His hand groped my breast and I felt his erection against my backside. I looked at Nermin with pleading eyes, but he was mesmerised by my naked flesh, his face flushed with desire.

'Please,' I begged. 'Please let me go.'

Karim was nuzzling my neck as his hands roamed my body.

'Senada,' I screamed. 'Senada, wake up.'

Karim covered my mouth with his hand and threw me on the bed. I scrambled to my feet while he undid his zipper.

'Please help me,' I begged Nermin.

His eyes jumped between Karim and me. 'Let her go,' Nermin said.

'What's wrong with you?' Karim slapped him on the arm. Nermin looked at me again, his eyes catching on my chest. Karim held me against him again. 'Look how beautiful she is. Don't you want her?'

Nermin tore his eyes away from me and looked at the floor. 'Not like this.'

'Aren't you fortunate?' Karim let me go and sat on the bed. 'I have a proposition for you.' He took a cigarette from his trouser pocket and lit up. 'You can choose one of us to marry.' He exhaled the cigarette languorously as if he had all the time in the world.

'And if I refuse,' I asked, wiping tears off my face.

'Then we will both have you,' Karim smiled.

I gasped and looked at Nermin.

'Happy my friend?' Karim asked him.

'Please, just let me go,' I cried.

'That is not the choice you were given,' Karim shouted, his face red with rage as he threw a chair to the floor.

I jumped in fear.

'Choose now or I will do it for you,' Karim demanded.

I looked at Nermin again.

'You heard him,' Nermin said. 'Make your decision.'

All the air was sucked out of the little room as my eyes danced between the two men. My fate was sealed the moment I decided to stay at the party. I lifted my arm and pointed.

'Congratulations my friend,' Karim said. 'You will make a beautiful couple.'

Nermin smiled, his face lit up with joy.

Suicide Watch

'Any problems with school?'

I shrugged, stifling a yawn.

'If you want to talk, I'm here to help.'

I barely restrained myself from rolling my eyes. Instead I slouched deeper into my chair and breathed out heavily, making my fringe lift and flop back onto my forehead. It was one lousy sentence that had condemned me to this. One lousy not-thought-out sentence.

When the principal had pulled me out of class a week ago while Miss Partridge, my English teacher, was instructing us on how to write an essay, I'd nearly had a coronary. This was the kind of attention a new student did not want. When we'd reached his office the principal had introduced me to Ms Malone, the high school counsellor.

'Please take a seat.' Ms Malone patted the chair next to her.

I sat awkwardly, trying to keep my body away from Ms Malone. I was so close I smelt her strawberry shampoo.

Ms Malone patted my arm. 'You've done nothing wrong.'

'We're here to talk to you about this.' Principal Papadopolous tapped a notebook.

I squinted and read the label upside down. It was my work experience diary. I gulped. Shit, they knew. That cow Vivian had dobbed me in.

In order to tell you about work experience I need to set the context, as Miss Partridge said in class. In the late sixth century Slavs moved down the Balkan Peninsula and established settlements. I'm just shitting you. I'm Bosnian. A few months ago that word would have meant nothing to you, but now that the Balkan War has broken out you don't need me to draw you a map, do you?

You're probably wondering what all this has to do with my work experience? Since the war my suburb has become like a mini-Yugoland with all the Bosnians streaming in. It used to my mum and me ever since my parents divorced when I was two years old and my dad went to live in Bosnia, but now it's like Tullamarine Airport at my house with the ethnics coming and going at all times of day and night.

Work experience had been my one chance to be normal and get rid of the ethnic baggage that's been dogging me like a bad smell since the war began. Instead people expected me to be Ray Martin and explain to them why there was a war.

I arrived at Jameson Investigative Services at 8.40 am. They'd told me that the starting time was 9.00 am, and I'd caught the early train. When I arrived the door was locked. I peered through the glass window and saw a woman behind the reception counter. I knocked.

The receptionist was doing her make-up and she looked up irritably from her compact. 'Can't you read?' she yelled. 'We open at nine.'

I hunched into my coat and crossed the street, peering through glass windows to kill time. I returned at 9.01 am on the dot. 'I'm here to see Mr Jameson,' I told the receptionist.

She looked at me without recognition. 'Take a seat.'

I sat, giving her a greasy. After ten minutes of sitting neatly and with my back straight so I made a good impression, I reached for my book and started reading.

Someone hit my shoulder. 'Didn't you hear me?' The receptionist stood over me. 'Mr Jameson is ready to see you.'

I saw the clock on the wall across from me. It was 9.30 am. I'd gotten so caught up in my book I'd lost touch with reality. 'Thanks.' I returned my book to my bag and stood. I didn't know where to go and looked at the receptionist. She pointed to a door on the left.

I pushed open the door and stood uncertainly in the doorway. The man behind the desk waved me in. 'Come in, Sabiha.' I approached the desk. 'Sit down.' He smiled at me. 'So you're here to do your work experience.'

'Yes.' I cleared my throat. 'I'm interested in finding out how to be a PI.' He gave me a blank look. 'Private Investigator,' I clarified.

He nodded and shuffled papers on his desk. 'And that's what we'll show you.' He lifted a sheet and read it. I shifted on my seat. He looked up. 'It's best if you spend time with Vivian.' He returned to the letter.

'Um, who's Vivian?'

'The receptionist.'

I waited to see if he had anything else to say. When he continued reading I stood and eased out of the office.

Approaching the reception area I could hear Vivian on the phone. 'Yeah, all right. I'll go pick up your helmet at lunch, but I'm not coming this weekend..... No, I'm not.... No I'm not.' I waited at the counter. 'Hang on,' she said into the headset. 'Yes?' She lifted her eyebrow at me.

'Mr Jameson asked me to help you today.'

Vivian stared at me stonily and I felt my stomach plunge. 'Typical,' she said and pressed a button on the switch. 'I'll call you back later.' She looked back at me. 'Did he say what you're supposed to help me with?'

I shook my head.

She tapped her fingers on the desk. Her face broke into a smile. 'Actually, you can help with a mailout.'

I spent the morning stuffing envelopes while Vivian answered the switchboard and pretended I wasn't there. It wasn't until three days later when we'd become friendly that I found out I was sending out debtor letters on behalf of finance companies who'd hired the company to track them down and get back their money.

They had to track down the debtors' address details using electronic white pages and electoral databases. That's why when I folded the letters for the envelope I had to hide the letterhead otherwise the debtors would see who it was from and throw it away unread.

At lunch she turned off the switch. 'I'll be back in an hour.'

I didn't know that I could eat my lunch at any time so it wasn't until three o'clock, when my stomach rumbled loud enough for Vivian to hear, that she told me to go on my lunch break.

That afternoon was the first time that the ethnic baggage made its reappearance. Vivian spent the afternoon organising for a meeting when Mr Smith arrived. Vivian went to notify Mr Jameson.

Mr Smith: 'Sabiha, that's an interesting name. Where are you from?'

Me: 'St Albans, in the western suburbs.'

Mr Smith: 'No.' He laughs. 'I mean which country.'

Me: 'Australia.'

Mr Smith: 'Your name isn't Australian.'

Me: 'It's Bosnian.'

Mr Smith: 'Ah, so you're Bosnian. Do you have family over there?'

Me: 'My aunt and grandfather came over here as refugees.'

Mr Jameson: 'Why is it happening? I mean you've all lived there in peace for years.'

Me: 'No, I didn't.'

Vivian returned and escorted Mr Smith into the boardroom. I pretended to be busy by re-typing a photocopying brochure so I didn't have to greet anyone else. When everyone arrived for the meeting Vivian told me to finish early because she was going to be taking minutes and couldn't supervise me.

I loved the train trip from home to the city, looking out the window as we passed by the industrial wasteland that marked the future that awaited the youth of western suburbs. Get a trade, get a factory job, break your back for the man and buy into the Aussie dream of a house with a backyard so you and hubby could chuck a barbie for your mates on the weekend while you're patting your pregnant tummy.

Going to the city I felt so superior. I was getting out, even if it was for work experience, I was getting out and for a few hours I could pretend I belonged in the hustle and bustle of the city. I could fool myself that I had a future and that I wasn't on the western suburbs production line toward adulthood.

I was escaping my home environment and Mum's mental health issues. She was released from hospital after her latest breakdown and the meds she took to regulate her Bipolar were flattening her. She didn't get off the couch where she slept most of the day away.

As the train passed each station from the city toward St Albans the illusion faded and once again I was a girl in a cheap K-Mart suit with shoes made of fake leather going back to where I belonged. I'd been staring out the window opposite and didn't realise it but the woman sitting across from me thought I was eyeballing her.

Old woman: 'Going home from work, dearie?'

Me: Nod.

Old woman: 'Me too. I'm going back home after a day out away from the neighbours.'

Me: Nod.

Old woman: 'They're terrible people. Bloody Greeks are trying to chase me out of my house so they can move in more of their family.'

Me: Eye the train door.

Old woman: 'They're trying to curse me. They put a white feather on my lawn. An evil white feather.'

Me: Run for the door as the train pulls into Ginifer station with the intention of changing carriages.

Old woman yells: 'Stay away from the Greeks.'

I made it into the next carriage as the old woman's warning filled my ears. She'd never have had this conversation with me if I'd looked like a real ethnic like my best friend Kathleen.

Nobody could mistake her for anything else with her dusky skin and dark brown eyes and hair. But with my blonde hair and blue eyes, people thought I was Anglo. As far as looks were concerned I could pass. It was only when people heard my name that they knew I wasn't one of them.

⁂

On Friday Tony, Vivian's boyfriend, arrived to take her to lunch while Vivian was in the toilet. I'd spent the past three days thinking through my answer to Mr Smith and I'd come up with a fool-proof plan to the dreaded question.

Tony: 'So you're Sabiha. Good to put a face to a name.'

Me: 'Yes, it is.'

Tony: 'So what nationality are you?'

Me: 'Australian-Bosnian.'

Tony: 'So which of your parents is Bosnian.'

Me: 'Both.'

Tony: 'So you're Bosnian.'

After he left I cursed under my breath. That option didn't work. I was going to have to try Plan C.

The second week of work experience Vivian was getting me to do other things for her. I was doing an inventory of the stationery cupboard so that she knew what to order when Mr Jameson walked past with an empty coffee cup. This was my opportunity to impress the boss and get in on some more exciting PI work.

Mr Jameson: 'I was curious. Where is your name from?'

Me: 'I'm Bosnian.'

Mr Jameson: 'You speak English so well. When did you come to Australia?'

Me: 'I was born here.'

Mr Jameson: 'So you're Australian.'

Me: 'I guess.'

I became deflated. I was never going to do anything but office jobs. I'd thought I was being so clever by not getting work experience at Target or McDonalds like my peers seeking a job. Now it turned out they were the smart ones.

Vivian's lunch breaks became longer, she came in later and left earlier because I was there to cover for her. She'd bring me little chocolates or buy lunch when she returned so I didn't mind much. Anyway, when she was away I had more reading time because the switchboard was usually dead between noon and two o'clock.

On one of her lunch breaks a courier delivered a parcel. After I signed and printed my name he lifted the clipboard and read my name out loud.

Courier: 'That's a cool name. Where's it from?'

Me: 'Bosnia.'

Courier: 'Wow, Boston. That's awesome.'

عُجِيو

A few days later Vivian went to buy express post envelopes from the post office, with a wink to indicate that she'd be taking her time. When Mrs Jameson arrived to take Mr Jameson to lunch, he was on the phone so I went into his office and slipped him a note.

When I returned the interrogation began.

Mrs Jameson: 'What nationality is your name?'

Me: 'Yugoslavian.'

Mrs Jameson: 'So which are you, Serbian, Croatian or Bosnian?'

This was even worse—someone who was actually informed about the ethnic mix of Yugoslavia.

Me: 'Bosnian.'

Mrs Jameson: 'So you're Muslim?'

Me: 'Yes.'

Mrs Jameson: 'Why aren't you covered up?'

Me: 'Bosnians don't cover up.'

Mrs Jameson: 'That's strange. I thought it was a Muslim thing.'

Me: 'It is.'

I didn't have it in me to explain that Bosnians never covered up because we had converted under the Turkish Ottoman Empire, but that would have led to more questions I was not qualified to answer.

Mr Jameson came and they left for lunch. 'It was nice talking to you, dear,' Mrs Jameson said as they left, her face puzzled.

۔مجھ

On Friday Vivian took me out to lunch to an Indonesian restaurant where I had a chicken stir-fry and a fried banana for dessert. God, that banana was delish. We'd been having a great time talking our arses off and I wasn't expecting it to happen with her too.

We were talking about our families. Vivian was Greek and she was telling me how her parents didn't like her boyfriend because he wasn't Greek. I was telling her about how things had changed since my mum's family came to live in Australia.

Me: 'Mum's acting like a born-again ethnic— '

Vivian: 'Don't use that word.'

Me: 'What?'

Vivian: She looked around before whispering, 'Ethnic.'

Me: 'Why? Everyone does.'

Vivian: 'It's a put-down.'

Me: 'I don't mean it as a putdown. It's what we are. We're ethnics.'

Vivian: 'No, we're Australian.'

We finished our lunch soon after that. I couldn't help but feel it was because of the ethnic thing. She handed me a basket of goodies that was delivered to the office as a thank you from a client which had fancy crackers, jam, and biscuits. I'd signed for the delivery and asked if it was alright for me to take it. 'He won't mind. He always regifts the baskets.'

Vivian called Mr Jameson and told him I was sick so she was taking me home and that she wouldn't be back for the day. Vivian had promised that there wouldn't be any problems with her lying, but now Principal Papadopolous and Ms Malone were putting me on the spot.

'Vivian said it was okay,' I told them. 'She said that since it was my last day and I'd done so much to help her I deserved a reward and could take the basket and leave early.'

Ms Malone smiled. 'And Vivian was right. You did really well at your work experience and received a glowing report from Mr Jameson.'

I let out a breath of relief.

'The reason we wanted to talk to you is because of this.' Ms Malone handed me a sheet of paper and I saw it was my reflection essay.

As part of the two weeks of work experience we had to keep a work diary of everything we did and then do a five-hundred word reflection on the experience.

Reflection by Sabiha Omerovic about work experience, 19 July 1994

I did my work experience at Jameson Investigative Services, 277 Sydney Road, Carlton, because I thought it would be interesting to learn about how to be a private investigator.

To be a private investigator you have to complete a six-month course at TAFE and then be supervised by another private investigator. But there are some investigators who don't do the course and learn on the job, like Mr Jameson.

I thought being a private investigator would be interesting because you'd do things like have to follow people and find out about them without them knowing. You'd also use technology and have to have good people skills so you could question people without them knowing and I think I'm good at using technology and talking to people.

In the two weeks that I did my work experience I learnt how to answer the phone, that you should use a sponge to make an envelope wet instead of licking it, how to fix a jammed photocopier and that working in an office is dead boring.

The only things I learnt about how to be a private investigator is that you use the white pages to find people's addresses and phone numbers and that when sending debtor letters you have to fold the envelope so that the letterhead can't be seen.

Having to sit at a desk all day and answer the phone made my back and neck ache and my eyes felt funny and dry, and at the end of the day I was really tired and had to go to bed at nine o'clock.

Vivian said my eyes were funny because the air con dries out the air and because staring at the computer screen all day irritates your eyes because the fluoro lights glare off the white screen. Vivian was the receptionist at Jameson Investigative Services and I worked with her the most.

I learnt from Vivian that being a receptionist sucks not only because it's boring but because you have to drink lots of water so your skin doesn't dry out from the air conditioning and so you need to go to the toilet a lot, but because you have to answer the phone all day you can't go to the toilet when you need to.

Vivian says that urinary tract infection is an occupational hazard and that she should get a tax rebate on her antibiotics because it is a workplace related injury but because she could never raise it with Mr Jameson, who is the boss, she'll have to suffer in silence and will probably be incontinent and infertile when she gets old.

I thought I would enjoy work experience more because it was a new place and no one knows what I am so that I could feel normal again but that didn't happen. I just want to disappear.

꙳

I re-read it and looked back at Ms Malone. 'I did everything Mr Green asked.' Mr Green was our careers counsellor and the one who helped us organise our work experience. 'He told us to talk about why we chose our particular profession and what we learnt from our work experience.'

'Your reflection is well written,' Ms Malone said. 'Slightly facetious, but overall you've met the criteria well. Our concern is with this.'

Ms Malone pointed to the last line. I re-read it and shrugged at her.

'Do you often feel like you want to disappear.'

'I guess,' I said.

And that was that. 'I just want to disappear,' at the end of my work experience reflection and after a conversation with my mum and about her mental health issues and suddenly I'm on suicide watch. I have to meet with Ms Malone, the high school counsellor and psychiatrist, once a week.

'Is there anything else you want to talk about?' Ms Malone asked.

I shook my head, having learnt when to keep my mouth shut.

Ms Malone closed her notebook. 'I'll see you next week.'

And another forty-five minutes of my life are down the drain.

Teddy

'You shouldn't have,' I said as my hands greedily caressed the textured wrapping paper. There was a card with my name, Lillian, written in cursive. I put it aside. It was my sixteenth birthday, or Sweet Sixteen as I'd called it whenever I'd talked about it in the past three months.

For a moment I held the box, holding onto the feeling of anticipation as I tried to imagine what was inside. I didn't expect much from Marie, who was my 'back up' friend. Our parents were best friends and we were forced into proximity at least once a month. I looked at the long box, my hands sliding on the lush wrapping paper. It was gold and almost felt like fabric under my searching hands. There was a big ribbon, carefully tied.

I'd received many presents in the past week leading up to my birthday. My real friends Trudy and Vanessa had bought me perfume in a carry bag. My parents, really my mum, had bought me clothes that she'd given me in a Target carry bag. I'd received a CD from my brother which he'd casually tossed at me while we'd watched TV, with an off the cuff, 'Happy birthday sis.'

Looking at the wrapping I tried to imagine what Marie could have bought. The box was long and shallow. I unobtrusively shook it as I placed it on my lap to unwrap and there was no sound. It had to be fabric, so some piece of clothing.

Marie cut out photos of lingerie model bodies and stuck photo cut-outs of her own head on top of them. She had a pretty face, but was perpetually on a diet claiming that if she just lost ten kilograms she would be happy with herself. I thought of her more as curvy, but whenever I said anything it fell on deaf ears so I'd given up.

With a deep breath I tore the wrapping paper and lifted the box lid. I folded back the tissue paper and stared at the contents, not understanding what I was looking at.

'It's a teddy,' Marie said, her hand caressing the black lace. 'You wear it as lingerie.'

I lifted the teddy out of the box. It was a black corset garment made of black lace and spandex, with wires on the side and under the breasts. The crotch had snaps to undo them with detachable shoulder straps.

'Those are for stockings.' Marie touched the detachable clips above the high-cut leg. I stood and held it up as she looked at the mirror, trying to imagine how it would look on. 'I'll turn around if you want to try it on.'

Marie and I'd had many sleepovers and I'd changed into pyjamas with her in the room, but to put this on I would have to get completely naked.

'I'll get us more snacks while you put it on.' Marie picked up the empty packet of chips and juice bottles on her desk and stepped out.

After I stripped naked I lifted the teddy over my head and tried to pull it on like a jumper. The tight lycra gripped my head, the wire in the side seams prevented me from pulling it all the way down and it got stuck on my held out arms.

I crouched over the bed and struggled out of it. I threw the teddy across the bed and it landed on the floor with a thud. With a sigh I jumped across the bed and got the teddy. I looked over the seams, trying to figure out how to get into it. The crotch had silver snaps in it. I unsnapped them and the crotch opened. I stepped into the teddy and pulled it up over my body. When the shoulder straps were on I snapped the crotch into place, my hand brushing against my pubic hair.

I ran over and looked in the mirror. It looked like I was poured into the teddy. The wire in the seams made it curve against my body accentuating my waist, while the cups lifted my boobs and squeezed them together as if I wore a push-up bra. 'Wow,' I whispered as I ran my hand over the lace panel on my torso.

There were stockings in the bottom of the gift box and I rolled them on, looking at myself as my bent leg rested on the bed. I looked like a seductress in a movie doing a lazy striptease. I rifled through Marie's closet and found her black high heels and walked up to the mirror.

'What are you looking at?' I whispered breathily, forming my mouth into a pout and bending so my boobs nearly popped out of the teddy.

There was a knock on the door. 'Hold on,' I shouted, taking Marie's dressing gown off the back of her chair and putting it on.

She opened the door. 'Come in, come in,' I whispered. I stalked to the door and yanked her in, taking the chips and lollies from her overflowing hands and closing the door before anyone could see me.

'How did you go?' Marie threw the snacks on the bed.

'Close your eyes,' I said.

Marie closed her eyes and waited. I undid the dressing gown and threw it on the bed, posing with my hands on my hips and my knee slightly bent. 'Open.'

Marie looked at me and gasped. 'Wow, you look beautiful, Lillian.' She walked to me and touched the lace teddy, her finger gently tracing the wire insert as it curved against my waist. 'So beautiful.' Her hand curved around my waist and suddenly she was so close.

She was taller than me and in the heels our eyes were level. Her brown eyes darkened with desire and she waited, asking permission. She leaned forward and I felt her warm breath on my lips.

'No,' I gasped, stepping away.

'Lillian.' Marie reached for my hand.

'Don't.' I yanked away. I threw on my jeans and jumper, bundling the rest of my clothes in the gift box. 'Let's go to the living room.' I didn't wait for her to speak as I walked to where our parents were socialising. I sat on the floor in front of the TV, the teddy cutting into my skin. This was my fault. Last weekend we were watching the movie *Never Been Kissed* when Marie said, 'I've never been kissed.'

I laughed, snorting my popcorn.

Marie looked hurt.

'You're not kidding!' I said.

Marie shook her head.

'In that case I'll be your first.' I leaned over and kissed her gently on the lips, keeping my mouth closed. 'Now you can say I'm your first.'

I didn't think twice about the kiss, just chalking it up to our usual mucking around, but Marie had obviously reached the wrong conclusion.

When we left her house an hour later, I avoided saying good-bye to Marie, instead stepping outside first and waiting for my parents to do their leave-taking. As we walked to the car Mum asked me what I'd gotten for my birthday present. I told her I got a top. When I got home I put the box in the back of my wardrobe and covered it with clothes.

That night I dreamt about the moment when Marie approached me and her hand curved around my waist. In my dream I didn't pull away, I let her place both hands on my waist, I waited with anticipation as she leaned in and kissed me, her lips sweet and soft. Her hands slipped the teddy off my shoulders. I woke up gasping, a liquid heat between my legs. I grabbed my pillow and held it against my face as I screamed into it. What was happening to me?

Over the next few months I avoided seeing Marie. Whenever her parents were due for a visit or my parents visited her, I always had plans with Trudy and Vanessa.

'Did something happen between you and Marie?' Mum asked me a few months after my birthday.

'No, we're just into different things.'

'I think you should make an effort. The two of you have known each other nearly your whole lives. You met at playgroup when you were three years old.'

'Just because you and her mum are friends doesn't mean we have to be,' I snapped.

Mum looked at me with concern, but didn't say anything else. As time passed Marie receded into my past, and my dreams of us dissipated like they had never been.

I'd forgotten about the teddy until months later when I was shopping with Trudy and Vanessa for our Year 10 formal.

'What about this?' Trudy asked coming out of the change room in a pink crinkle dress that highlighted her every bulge.

'It's nice.' I turned my face away. Trudy and I were in the debating club with Michael and we'd both fallen for his black curly hair, tall lithe frame and the heartfelt poems he published on his blog.

Usually when it came to boys I was happy for Trudy to take the lead, but this time I was gripped with desperation. I needed to be with Michael. I needed him to take away the memory of Marie. Our arguments about Michael had nearly broken our friendship group, until Vanessa intervened and we came to an agreement—we'd let Michael pick at the formal.

'I'm not sure it does you justice,' Vanessa said.

I cursed under my breath as Trudy returned to the dressing room. I found a black velvet dress and tried it on. I was looking at myself in the mirror when Trudy approached in another tight-fitting dress. 'You have to wear a bra with that one, Lillian.' She pointed at the cleavage. The v-neckline covered my breasts.

'The bra straps will be visible.' Vanessa stared at my bare back.

'I'll take it,' I said to the sales girl.

I knew by Trudy's smile that she thought she'd won, but she didn't know about the teddy. As we spent the afternoon going from shop to shop I was in an agony of anticipation. I couldn't wait to get home and try on the teddy and dress together.

When I got home and locked the door to my bedroom, I pulled out the teddy and looked at myself in the mirror. I needed more make-up. I wiped off the lipstick with a tissue and put on foundation, black eyeliner and mascara, and then the red lipstick. As I pulled up the dress over my hips I felt a thrill of anticipation. I looked so sophisticated and womanly. I knew that Michael's eyes wouldn't move off me all night.

I imagined dancing with Michael, my arms lifted on his shoulders, my breasts pressed up against his chest. I moved my legs in small steps, the tight dress restricting my movements and making them slow and languid.

I puckered my lips and looked at myself in the mirror. I touched myself, my hands rubbing against the velvet, caressing my body underneath. The skin on top of my breasts was so soft. I squeezed the firm flesh, watching the way my fingers sunk into my skin. I imagined Michael squeezing my breasts as he kissed me, his fingers caressing my nipples.

I lay on the bed and kept touching myself, pretending Michael was over me. I glanced at the mirror and watched myself, my face was shiny from sweat and my eyes heavy lidded. I moaned as I came, my eyes closing and in the blackness I saw Marie's face as she leaned down to kiss me, her eyes full of desire. My eyes snapped open and I watched the ceiling as I lay against the bed.

I wondered what she was doing? An ache of loneliness swept over me. For so many years she had been a part of my life, someone whose presence I took for granted, but now I missed her comforting shoulder. The way her nose wrinkled when she was listening hard, or the way she was tactile and placed her hand on my arm when I was upset. I had to stop this. I got up from the bed and briskly changed into my regular clothes. Marie was in the past. Michael was my future. I looked at the clock. I had to get to Trudy's house.

When I arrived Trudy was wearing a bathrobe that didn't close properly revealing pink lace bra and panties.

'Lillian, you can change in the bathroom,' Vanessa said after we'd hugged. We'd decided to get ready at Trudy's house because she had her own bathroom and we could share make-up.

'That's all right.' I toed off my runners and undid my jeans. I bent over in the teddy and looked for my robe.

'Where did you get that?' Trudy demanded.

'It was a birthday present.' I tied my robe so that the teddy was still exposed. Picking up my make-up bag I headed for the bathroom.

'Who got it for you?' Trudy followed.

'A friend.' I put on my foundation and outlined my eyes with liquid eyeliner.

'What friend? You never mentioned anyone before.'

I looked into my make-up bag, pretending to search for lipstick. I hadn't anticipated this response and was flustered about what to say. I didn't want to tell them Marie had bought it for me or they'd call me a lesbo.

'If a guy gives lingerie as a present he expects to see it worn.' Trudy's face was red and her voice full of spite.

'Maybe he will tonight.'

Trudy gasped. 'Michael gave you that for a present,' she shrieked. I shrugged. 'Slut,' she whispered under her breath.

Vanessa pulled her out of the bathroom and I heard them whispering. I had declared my crush on Michael a few months ago and as usual Trudy had announced her crush on him. Even though I was hands down prettier, she'd snapped up all the guys I'd liked for the past six months because she went all the way. But that was going to change tonight.

'Don't let her get to you. You know she's just jealous.' Vanessa touched my shoulder.

I snapped my compact closed. 'I won't.'

When we arrived at the reception centre where our formal was held I slowed my steps so that Trudy and Vanessa went ahead of me. As I walked through the entrance I felt everyone looking at me. I'd practiced my walk, ensuring my back was straight and my hips swayed. I knew that Trudy would make a beeline for Michael.

'Lillian said that you bought her a teddy,' I heard Trudy saying to Michael as I approached.

'No, Trudy,' I interrupted. 'I said I'd received the teddy as a birthday present and that I was wearing it for Michael.' I met his gaze and channelled all the desire I'd felt as I touched myself while wearing the teddy.

His eyes widened and he took a deep breath. 'Would you like to dance?'

As we swayed against each other his sweaty hand rubbed up and down my back, goosepimples raised on my skin as the cool air hit the damp patches he left behind. He bent his head and kissed me, his teeth grazing against my lips, while his thick tongue pushed into my mouth.

I had to fight against stiffening in his arms. This always happened when I was with a boy. I dreamt about being with him for months and then the minute we got together, I felt revulsion and couldn't wait to get away from him.

I put my arms around his neck and pressed myself against him. This time I wasn't backing off and letting Trudy win. I knew I'd get into it and all the feelings of desire I felt when I dreamt about Michael would return.

Michael lifted his head. 'Let's get out of here.' He pulled me toward the exit. I hesitated. I knew that if I walked out with him I was telling Michael it was okay. But I wasn't sure it was. I wasn't sure this was what I wanted.

Before I knew it we were in the gardens outside the reception centre. Michael led us deep into the foliage and leaned me against a tree as he kissed me. I kissed him back. It was a beautiful balmy night and the moonlight lit up the garden around us.

I yearned to feel something and for a moment I thought it was working. I felt a faint stirring between my legs as Michael gripped my arse and lifted me against him. But then he pushed me against the tree and the bark cut into my back. I broke the kiss. 'Ouch,' I muttered, trying to push him away.

'Let me see the teddy,' he whispered as his tongue swirled around my earlobe.

His wet saliva covered my ear. He was ruining it all. This was supposed to be a sexy romp, instead it was becoming a gross-fest. I remembered the way I'd prepared for this night, watching myself in the mirror as I touched myself, getting hotter. I knew what I had to do.

'Move away and I'll show you.' I pushed Michael and took a step back. I danced to the soundtrack in my head, moving my hips as my hands moved over my body. I pushed the dress over my shoulders and coyly looked at Michael from under my eyelashes.

He followed me with his eyes as he panted slightly. He reached for my breasts but I slapped them away. I pushed the dress down my hips and stepped out of it. 'You are so beautiful, Lillian,' he muttered as he grabbed me and mashed his lips to mine.

'No.' I tried to push him away, finally breaking my lips away. 'It's not supposed to be like this.' He put his hand between us and undid his pants. His fingers were between my legs, clumsily poking and pinching as he tried to pull off my panties. 'Stop it. You're hurting me.' I pushed his hand away.

His hand gripped mine and he pushed it onto his penis, moving it up and down as he made me stroke him. I moaned at his tight grip and he squirted all over my hand. He got a hanky from his pocket and wiped my hand. 'Sorry I got so out of control,' he said, as his hands caressed the teddy. 'You just drove me crazy in that outfit.' He kissed me and I felt his erection grow again.

'Not now.' I pulled up my dress.

'Next time I'll give you the whole treatment.' He leaned down and kissed the top of my breast. He put his arm around my waist and led me back to the reception centre. I felt everyone's eyes on us as we swayed to the slow music under the disco ball. 'Are you having a good time?' Michael kissed my cheek.

'It was everything I dreamt about.'

He smiled and pulled me closer to him. Above us the disco ball turned, the reflected light circling around and around.

'Bathroom break.' I tore myself out of Michael's grasp. I passed the bathroom and left the reception centre. As I walked down the driveway I got my mobile out of my handbag and pressed Marie's phone number. The phone rang. Joy filled me as I heard Marie's voice saying hello. 'It's Lillian. I'm so sorry. I was scared to face the truth. I want to be with you.'

There was silence on the other end. Was she going to hang up on me?

'Hello, Marie. Are you there?' I finally said.

'Yes, I'm here. Where are you?'

I told her the name of the reception centre. 'I'm at the end of the driveway. I'm going to try and call a taxi.'

'Wait there. I'll come pick you up.' She hung up.

I spent the next ten minutes walking up and down the sidewalk of the street, waiting. The reception centre was lit up and I heard my fellow classmates laughing and dancing as they stood in the foyer, taking photos of themselves and chatting to each other in the quiet. I had spent so much time wanting to be a part of the group, willing to do anything just to blend in, and yet now I wanted to get as far away as possible. There was only one person who mattered.

A white car pulled up, Marie's brother in the driver's seat. She stepped out of the passenger seat and walked to me. I fell into her arms, shivering from cold and shock. Feeling her warm body pressed against mine was like coming home.

She sat on the backseat beside me as her brother drove us home, the streetlights flickering over Marie's smiling face. I gripped her hand tight.

The Heart of the Matter

The receptionist nodded to the door on my left. 'The doctor will see you now.'

I stood and smoothed down my school dress. The surgery was three houses away from my school so I'd made an appointment after school finished. I walked into the doctor's office and closed the door behind me.

The doctor raised her eyebrows and adjusted her glasses. 'Your parents?' she asked and I shook my head.

This whole thing could go south in a hurry if I had brought my migrant parents with me. My friend Selma was going to come with me, but something came up at the last moment. I wondered if my parents had been talking to her, or maybe Selma was busy with her boyfriend. Being five years older she was supposed to be playing the adult and now I had to wing it with the doctor. So much for me being the little sister she never had.

The doctor motioned for me to sit and looked at my referral letter. 'Where is the scar?' she asked as if the referral letter didn't tell her that.

I undid the buttons of my school uniform and the doctor saw what only a few people have seen. There in full view was the memento of my defective heart and the operation to correct it when I was two years old. The long raggedy scar dissected my chest in two as if I was struck by a knight's sword. It stretched from my collarbone to belly button, but as I grew it shrunk a bit until it reached the end of my ribcage. When we were little I let my younger brother touch the jagged line once and he said it felt like squashed blue tack under his fingers. That was the result of the scar tissue thickening and thinning at different parts like a river on a map.

Shortly after puberty hit and my boobs grew, I wore cowl necked t-shirts and turtleneck tops only. This didn't stop a boy from my street asking me out. He was cute and I said yes. It was early summer and the afternoon was warm so I punched my inner demon in the face and put on a V-necked top.

We ate ice cream and just when I thought I was safe the boy asked, 'What's that on your chest?'

'I had a heart operation when I was little,' I'd said, nervously tugging on my t-shirt.

'Really, shit.' His words created another scar on top of my real one. A few minutes later I walked home by myself, my t-shirt bunched in my hand over the scar. One thought throbbed in my head. The scar had to go.

'Can anything be done?' I asked the doctor.

The doctor gently pressed on the top of it, the thickest section where the surgeon had struggled to insert the scalpel that would slice my skin.

She made some notes on my file, lifted her head and said, 'Nothing.'

I would have preferred if she slapped me because that would explain my tears.

Seeing my watering eyes she softened slightly. 'Just keep it out of the sun,' she said, taking note of my tan. 'That makes it worse.'

The moment I left the office anger rose inside me like a tsunami. Like I didn't know that the scar couldn't tan. Like I didn't know that if I stayed in the sun it would just go red like someone drew a line with red texta on me.

'She probably thought you were a time-waster who didn't have money to do anything,' Selma said later, stretching her gum in a very non-adult like fashion. Ever since she had a nose job she was more aloof and confident at the same time. She had fallen on her honker when she was little and her nose stayed crooked for the next fifteen years until she finally fixed it last year. Now that she had a little Betty Boop nose no one could get her on the phone anymore. She was either out or talking to someone. She underwent a metamorphosis from a girl sucking on her collars to a true-blue social butterfly.

Around this time my stepfather kicked up a notch in his everyday teasing which in his younger days was a way of bonding. He'd trotted out jokes in Bosnian like: *'Koliko je sati?,'* which meant 'What time is it?' Sometimes he asked me riddles that were meant to be funny like: 'Did you see the movie *Baldies are Pulling their Hair,*' or 'Did you see the movie *A Dry Rag At the Bottom of the Sea.*'

'Look at your nose,' he'd point. 'People would think you're my daughter.' My stepfather had a honker of a nose, a common Bosnian trait, and he'd learnt early in his life that the easiest way to deal with your foibles was to acknowledge them yourself.

'Shut up,' I'd shout, rushing out of the room and slamming the door.

That night I covered the mirror in my room with a bed sheet. Every time my reflection stared back at me it was like I had become Pinocchio who had told another lie.

My mother was on the phone to Selma's parents while I tugged on her shirt. 'What kind of friend does this?' she yelled and waved the letter from the hospital with the date and time of my operation.

Selma had finally come through and via her boyfriend's connection arranged a plastic surgeon that agreed to the operation after my seventeenth birthday. The surgery was booked for four days after my birthday. All I needed to do now was to climb Mount Everest, which in my world was known as getting parental approval. I had been softening my mother up for some time and now I went for the kill.

'You said that you hated your nose when you were young so you know how I feel. Please Mum I want to feel normal,' I pleaded while holding the handset down so she couldn't dial Selma's parent's number again.

'You are normal,' Mum said.

'Come on, tell me it's not big.'

Mum's eyes drifted to my nose and her silence spoke volumes. She went to the kitchen and started cleaning. Later that night while I was brushing my teeth she came and said, 'All right, if it will make you happy.'

I gave her a kiss and a hug, toothpaste foam and all.

'About the money,' she said and in a long breathless sentence I told her how I had saved all of my AUSTUDY payments and my income from frying chips at Hungry Jacks where I worked part-time. After we sorted out financials I went to my room and took the bed sheet off my mirror.

Caught up with the heady thought of my impeding transformation I examined my body critically. My knees were too big for my legs and had to be altered. I didn't know if this could be done, but I would ask about it. My ankles jutted out like knobs, and I had a sticky out stomach that no amount of sit-ups affected. I sucked in my stomach and admired the concave curve. I added stomach liposuction to my list.

The surgery went as scheduled and I woke up afterwards feeling drowsy. My nose was packed with bandages and I had to breathe through my mouth. My eyes were dry and hurting. I couldn't eat or drink anything for four hours because it might cause me to vomit, and if I did vomit I would tear my stitches. A nurse placed a bedpan on the bedside table next to me just in case, and warned me not to swallow the blood pouring down the back of my throat. I understood the precautions, but I was so thirsty it was a physical pain. I begged for water and was finally allowed to sip small amounts.

I needed to go to the toilet and rang for a nurse.

'Here you go, love.' She placed a bedpan on the bed next to me.

'No, I want to go to the toilet.'

'You can't,' the nurse said. 'It's not safe.'

'But I have my period,' I whispered.

'Other patients have their period.' Her matter-of-fact attitude dumbfounded me.

'I'll get blood on the bed.'

'It doesn't matter.' She closed the curtains.

I put the bedpan on the bed and manoeuvred myself on top of it. I was wearing a hospital gown that was open at the back and had an IV drip in my arm. As I arranged myself to crouch over the bedpan I felt dizzy and had to hold onto the bed so I didn't topple over.

After I peed the nurse came and took the bedpan away. I lay back in bed and slept again. When I awoke next it was late at night and my bladder was full. This time I knew better than to call the nurse. I slowly got out of the bed and shuffled to the bathroom, pushing along my IV.

After I finished I opened the stall door. In front of me was a mirror. I looked up and gasped. There was a girl staring at me. She had bandages across her forehead and nose, her face swollen and bruised like someone beat her up. Then the girl in the mirror realised that she did it to herself.

My tears soaked the bandages adding to my discomfort. All my fantasies that I would be beautiful after my nose job were a lie. I was more hideous than I'd been before the nose job. I was terrified that I was maimed for life and would look like a horrible monster everyone would make fun of.

The nurse heard me crying. 'It's just swelling,' she said. 'It will go down.'

I gulped down tears, wanting to believe her, but still suspicious that any of this could end in a good news story.

After I was released I spent the new few days lying on the couch, drinking painkillers every four hours that sent me into a dream state where the future and past didn't exist. I was like Sleeping Beauty, waiting for the right time to awaken.

Two weeks later, back to school, I implemented my makeover plan. I cut my hair short and dyed it brown myself. I'd imagined that my face would go dramatically lighter and my green eyes would stand out more, instead there was only a slight change. On the morning of my return to school I carefully put on make-up and dressed nicely, feeling excited about my debut. I'd sworn my girlfriends to secrecy and expected that I would blend into the normal school day.

As soon as I walked onto the school grounds, I knew someone had squealed. There were curious looks and nudges as I walked past. We were in our home economics theory class preparing our meal plans. There was jostling at the table across from ours and Emre came to kneel down beside me.

'You got a nose job?' he asked.

'Yes.' I stared at the table, avoiding his eyes.

'Hurt much?'

'Yeah, I had to take painkillers for a few days.'

'It looks good.'

I looked up and met his eyes for the first time and smiled.

He returned to his group and some of the boys pointed at me and others nodded. One of them whistled. I turned toward the group and he put his thumb up. The bomb I expected to go off was defused. There would be no teasing or talk behind my back.

That night when I looked myself in the mirror I was pleased with the girl looking back at me, but my eyes kept coming back to the scar on my chest. I opened my wardrobe and ran my fingers across all the open neck tops, dresses and shirts. Maybe I could wear them if I could somehow cover my scarred skin. I tried various necklaces but it seemed that my eyes were even more drawn to my chest. I went to the laundry and tore off a large plastic garbage bag from the roll. Back in my room I filled it with all the clothes I wouldn't be wearing again: singlets, v-necks and bottle necked tops... all of it went into the darkness of the black bag. I took the bag to the garage and stuck a sticker that I wrote 'donation' on.

A year later I returned to the doctor's surgery for my annual check up. I was flicking through a magazine when I read an article by a woman who became a paraplegic after a car accident and ended up in a wheelchair.

Whenever she was in public she faced questions from strangers who thought it was appropriate to ask her life story, because her point of difference was visible. For years she went along with it, feeling that the polite thing to do was play along. Most times the minute people found out her story, the conversation was over. They'd intruded on her personal life, made her relive a painful personal hurt over and over, just for their rude curiosity, until the day she had an epiphany that she didn't owe anyone anything, certainly not her life story.

One day while in an elevator with a stranger they did the usual courteous dance of who would press the button, and then stared at the door in front of them as the elevator climbed floors. She noticed the curious stares the stranger was giving her wheelchair.

'So, how did you end up in a wheelchair?' he asked.

'That's my personal business,' she answered calmly.

The man turned red and stammered. 'I was just making conversation,' he defended himself.

'That's not an appropriate topic of conversation,' she said.

He got out on the next floor, avoiding eye contact with her.

The receptionist called my name and I returned the magazine back to the coffee table where I'd found it, but the woman's story never left me.

Selma and her boyfriend took me out for dinner to celebrate my new look. She revealed that she was engaged and her new fiancé added that the engagement ring was on the way. During dinner I thanked him for pulling strings and organising the appointment with the plastic surgeon.

'No dramas. I'm sure he'd be happy to take a look at your scar,' Selma's boyfriend said while chewing a piece of meat.

I sent a thousand-dagger stare at Selma, but in her love-drunk state she was oblivious to my anger. What's more she said, 'Let him have a look.' She touched the collar of my shirt. 'They can do miracles these days.'

I ripped my shirt open and a button flew off landing on the table.

'Bloody hell.' Selma's fiancé nearly choked, 'that is a freakin'...'

'Just a scar,' I enunciated, staring at him.

His eyes widened slightly, before he quickly broke eye contact and looked down at his plate.

I ran out of the restaurant. It took me nearly an hour to get home and my throat was dry and burning, my eyes itchy from the wind, but I felt no pain or tiredness. Maybe I flew home. I ran to the garage and found my black bag. In my room I took out my clothes and returned them back to my wardrobe.

My mother walked in and asked me if I was all right.

'Never better.' I ran into her embrace.

Friends Forever

'How are you this morning, Mrs James?' the nurse asked as she fluffed my pillow.

'All right, dear.' She was new and had that fresh scrubbed look of youth. Her voice was cheerful and slightly high-pitched as if she were speaking to a toddler. 'Please call me Gertrude.'

'What about you, Mrs Hassleback?' She tucked the sheet around Shirley and fluffed her pillow. Shirley stared blankly at her.

The nurse's composure broke for a moment. Shirley's stare had a habit of doing that to people, at least until you got used to it. Most Alzheimer patients looked blank. As if the lights were switched off in their brain, but not Shirley.

She looked like there was a part of herself fighting to come back. Her eyes were full of terror. Like there was something horrific only she could see and she was screaming for help, but she couldn't get any part of her body to cooperate.

'Shirley's fine,' I told the nurse.

The nurse nodded and scuttled from the room.

'You've done it again, Shirley.' I laughed. 'You have to stop scaring them off.'

Anne, our regular nurse, came in and handed me my medication. 'Here you go.'

I swallowed it in one hit and chased it with water.

'How was your night?' Anne asked. 'Were you in pain?'

I shook my head. I was lying. It was getting hard to breathe but I didn't want them to up the pain medication and turn me into a vegetable. I had to be alert for Shirley.

'Maybe today will be the day?' Anne nodded at Shirley.

'Maybe.'

Anne helped me out of bed and to the bathroom. After I'd finished my ablutions I dressed in my visiting clothes. Even though Shirley and I lay beside each other every day and, had done so for the past five years, I wanted it to be special. Today might be the day that she returned to the real world and I wanted to greet her in style.

When I returned to the room Anne had set up the armchair. After I sat she handed me my glasses and notebook. 'Thank you, dear,' I said when she placed the buzzer on the armrest.

I held the closed notebook in my lap. I'd read it so many times I didn't need to open it, but it comforted me to hold it. 'It's been fifty years,' I told Shirley. 'Fifty years since our friendship began.'

I closed my eyes. The pain had muted to a dull roar after the medication Anne had administered, but sitting in the armchair aggravated my muscles. Still I had to sit face-to-face with Shirley. It only worked if I could see her eyes.

'We went to the same school, but it wasn't until we started working at Dr Metcalfe's surgery that we became friends.' I opened my eyes. Shirley's frozen stare was unchanged.

'In high school we'd been in opposite cliques. I was the butcher's daughter and you were the daughter of a lawyer. To you the job at Dr Metcalfe's was a chance to save pin money for your European tour. For me it was a job that would set me up for life.'

~؎~

The first time I saw Shirley I hated her on sight. She'd walked into the surgery in a pink twin-set and flowing pink skirt, her blonde hair curled around her heart shaped face, the faintest sheen of pale pink lipstick shimmering on her lips. 'I'm here about the job,' she'd said in her girly voice.

I'd nodded curtly and called Dr Metcalfe. As the doctor fawned over her I smoothed my tweed skirt and pushed my lank brown hair behind my ears. I'd always known I wasn't pretty and it had never bothered me before. I was the progeny of two ordinary people who valued hard work and loyalty over superficiality like nice clothes and pretty hair.

But working side-by-side with Shirley made me excruciatingly aware of my lack of feminine wiles. All of the patients directed their queries to her and I became invisible. Her sweet smile and gentle manner made me seem curt and abrupt. After the first day I left the counter to her and instead did the filing.

'Let me help you, Gertrude,' Shirley said during a lull in the waiting room. She took half of the stack of filing and sorted them. 'How long have you worked here?'

'A year.' I hadn't finished high school. There had been no point.

The bell over the door rang as someone entered the waiting area. I kept filing. When I heard my name called I looked up. Stephen held out the lunch I'd forgotten at the butcher shop.

Shirley was looking at his butcher's apron with her small nose wrinkled. It was streaked with blood after a morning's work. I walked past her and took my lunch box from him, pulling him in for a quick kiss on the lips. He smiled shyly.

'Your boyfriend?' Shirley asked after he left.

'Fiancé.' I finished the filing. 'I'm going to lunch.' I picked up my lunch box and left.

I knew people like her looked down on people like me and Stephen. She came from money and had gotten the job because her father and Dr Metcalfe were friends. I had earned the job based on my excellent academic record and reliability.

I shifted on the armchair again, trying to find a more comfortable place. 'Do you remember Shirley?' I peered into her frozen eyes, looking for a spark of recognition. 'We were like chalk and cheese. We would have remained like that until the end of summer. Co-workers who barely tolerated each other if it wasn't for June Davis. Who would have thought that two women with so little in common were so much alike?'

June Davis was the fast girl in our small country town, or at least she was according to the boys who bragged about her when they were alone. She was one of those girls who exuded sex appeal. Her breasts had developed when she was fourteen and she'd received constant attention from men young and old.

We'd been working together for a few weeks in cold civility when June Davis stumbled into the waiting room with blood dripping down her thighs. I saw her first and ran to catch her before she collapsed onto the cold floor. Shirley called Dr Metcalfe and helped me half carry June into the surgery.

'I didn't want to,' she kept whispering as we helped her onto the exam table.

'What happened?' Dr Metcalfe asked.

'The Baker twins forced me.' June started to cry.

The Baker twins were the reverend's sons.

'I'm sure you're wrong,' Dr Metcalfe said. 'You must have given them the wrong idea. Girls, leave,' he told Shirley and me.

Shirley headed for the door. I stood beside June and pulled her into a hug.

'Leave now.' Dr Metcalfe commanded me.

Shirley stopped.

'No.' I defiantly returned his stare. I knew what he planned to do. He was going to bully June into thinking she was the one to blame. After a cursory examination he would force her to go home and keep quiet about what had happened.

'Leave or you will be fired,' Dr Metcalfe said.

'I won't let June become another Mary Smith.'

Mary Smith was a girl who had committed suicide by hanging herself in the woods. It was whispered that she'd been in trouble. Only four people knew the truth of what had happened. Dr Metcalfe, the Baker boys and me.

Shirley picked up the phone. 'I'll call Daddy,' she said.

'There's no need for that,' Dr Metcalfe reached to take the phone from her hand.

'Yes, there is,' Shirley said.

Dr Metcalfe retreated. Shirley grimly smiled at me and dialled. That was the end of our jobs at Dr Metcalfe's surgery and the beginning of our friendship.

Nothing happened to the Baker boys. Nothing ever happened to boys like them. They were the pillars of the community and June was the girl who'd been around, but there were no more girls like June or Mary, at least not in our town. The reverend packed up and moved three months later. The whispers got too much for him.

'Do you remember what happened afterwards?' I asked Shirley. 'Dr Metcalfe had more influence than either one of us had realised. The way he told the story June had entrapped the poor Baker boys and we'd supported her vicious lies.'

In the months afterward Shirley and I had drawn together as the town turned on us. Shirley told me about her boyfriend, Troy. He was a lawyer like her father and he wanted them to go together to Europe for their honeymoon. She wanted the trip to be her great adventure before she married, but she feared that if she didn't marry Troy, he wouldn't wait for her.

I told her about Stephen. We'd been together since we were twelve and had our lives together planned out. I would run the business side of our shop, while he managed the shopfront. We would have saved enough to open our own shop if I'd kept working at Dr Metcalfe's, but now our plans were set back.

We'd meet at the Davis' cafe. June's parents were grateful for how we'd helped her and they always had a table available for us in the backroom. After a while Stephen and Troy hung around with us and we became a foursome.

'Any luck?' Shirley asked as she placed the milkshakes on the table.

I shook my head. 'Apparently there are no vacancies at the factory.'

Shirley rolled her eyes. The canning factory was the biggest employer in our area and they had started their annual recruitment a few weeks ago, but as a *persona non grata* I was unemployable.

'Maybe my dad can give you a job?' She'd started working for her father after Dr Metcalfe fired us, even though there was no official work and he was making up jobs for her to do. 'We can share. I can give you half my hours.'

Before I knew her I would have thought she was making an empty gesture. 'It's okay.' I sipped my milkshake. 'Something will turn up.'

'What about your wedding?'

We couldn't get married until we'd saved enough for the shop. A married woman was instantly off the job market.

'We have all the time in the world.' Stephen and I were only twenty years of age and had our whole lives ahead of us, or at least it seemed like that at the time. 'What about you and Troy?'

They'd been fighting a lot lately about her wanting to travel by herself. 'I don't know. Maybe I should just get married.' She finished her milkshake, making a slurping sound as she sucked the last of it through the straw.

'Will you be happy?'

Shirley shrugged. 'I know I don't want to lose him.'

'There they are,' I nodded toward the cafe door.

Troy and Stephen walked in together. Tonight was the annual town dance and we were all going together in one car.

The two men were wearing suits. Troy's was obviously quality and fitted him like a glove. When he came to stand beside Shirley in her pink satin dress they looked like a Hollywood glamour couple. Stephen wore his brother's suit which fitted him loosely, a navy tie around his neck. I wore a navy dress patterned with yellow daisies. Alone we looked like bean polls, but together we looked tall and athletic.

We were going in Troy's car. Stephen and I sat in the back. Stephen put his hand on my knee, his broad hand feeling coarse from the scrubbing to remove the blood. I placed my hand over his and squeezed. Shirley was chattering away in the front. Troy nodded as he drove, his arm on the back of the seat and hugging her shoulders.

When we arrived at the hall there were cars parked for miles around. We had to park far away and walk. Shirley got out of the car and groaned as her heels sunk into the dirt. I smiled and looked away. I'd warned her not to wear her dainty shoes but she hadn't listened.

'Let me help,' Troy scooped her up in his arms and carried her toward the hall. Shirley giggled and kicked her legs.

Stephen and I walked behind them, our arms around each other's waist, our strides perfectly matched. When we walked into the hall a hush descended. Shirley and I looked at each other. We'd worried that even here we'd be ostracised but Troy and Stephen hadn't let us back out. The Desperate and Dateless Ball was the only social event in our small town.

Within an hour alcohol had loosened everyone's inhibitions and we were able to blend in with the crowd. Stephen drank more than usual and Troy joined him, matching him beer for beer.

'You're the designated driver,' Troy slurred after his fifth beer.

'You should have told me that earlier,' Shirley snapped, putting down her champagne glass.

Stephen let loose and by the end of the night we all had to help him to the car. When Shirley started driving she ground the gears and looked at Troy, waiting for him to snap at her. He sat in the passenger seat and smiled goofily.

'You're such a bad driver.' He fell asleep and was snoring by the time we reached town.

Shirley dropped me off first and Stephen stepped out of the car, and I had to catch him from falling onto the grass. 'Goodnight my love.' He kissed me on the lips. I blushed, aware of Shirley's eyes upon us. I helped him back into the car and closed the car door.

I waved from my driveway and as they drove away, Stephen hung halfway out the window and shouted, 'I love you.' I laughed and whispered, 'I love you too,' not wanting to wake my parents, my lips still tingling from his kiss.

There was a knock on the door and Anne appeared. 'They're here,' she said, nodding toward Shirley. 'Should they come in.'

I closed my notebook and sighed. 'I don't think today will be a good day.' I put my glasses on the table beside me and went to stand up, wincing as pain cut through me. Anne approached and helped me up. I walked from the bedroom into the hallway.

'Hello Auntie Gertrude,' a tall middle-aged man with Shirley's blue eyes greeted me.

'Hello Artie. Good to see you. And look at your beautiful children.' His daughter and son were next to him. We spent a few minutes exchanging smalltalk.

'Do you think we could see her today?' Artie nodded toward the door.

'I'm worried today is going to be one of those tough days, but of course you decide. I'll be there to smooth over troubled waters.'

On her bad days Shirley couldn't remember anyone and viewed everyone as a stranger who wished her harm. She was like a feral cat scratching and hissing at anyone who approached her.

Artie looked from the door to me. 'That's okay. We'll just drop some goodies off for her.' He handed me a shopping bag with containers in it.

'I'll serve these to her and tell her they're from you. Who knows, it might spark a memory.'

Artie nodded and gave me a quick kiss on the cheek.

I walked down the hall and into another resident's bedroom. Poor Colleen didn't have any visitors in the five years I'd been at the nursing home. 'Look dear, your son came to drop off some goodies for you.' I took out the containers and placed them on her bedside table.

'He came.' Colleen's face brightened.

'Of course. Your son loves you. He visits you every week. You were just having one of your episodes while he was here so you don't remember.' I sat on the chair next to Colleen's bed and served her the pavlova that Artie had brought, telling her elaborate lies about her son and grandchildren.

The light came back into Colleen's eyes as I spoke and a wave of benevolence filled me. I was a good person.

After Colleen ate and I wiped her face I returned to the room I shared with Shirley.

'Where was I?' I asked as I opened my notebook. 'That's right. It was the night of the Desperate and Dateless Ball. You and Troy had dropped me off.' I closed my eyes and saw Stephen's smiling face as he waved at me through the back window. 'I will always regret not shouting back.' I peered into Shirley's eyes. They looked to be clearing, as if she was waking from a dream. 'In the days afterward you were a true friend to me,' I told her.

'I didn't know that Stephen hadn't made it home until his brother came to my house in the morning looking for him. They found his body beside their garage. The police concluded that after you and Troy dropped him off Stephen was stumbling toward the house when someone struck him down in his own driveway. Later people told of seeing one of the Baker boys, but nothing was ever proven.'

I knew that she was coming back to the real world, but her face remained immobile. She was pretending she wasn't aware.

'Can you believe how things turned out?' I asked Shirley, not expecting a response and not getting one. 'After Stephen died I wanted to die along with him, but the body was unwilling even if the spirit was ready. You and Troy put your lives on hold to support me. A year later you went to Europe by yourself and never came back. Troy became my only friend and he kept asking me to marry him, until three years after Stephen died, I agreed.'

I waited for her to speak up, but she was still playing possum.

'You didn't return back home after Europe. For a few years you sent me postcards from different parts of the world while Troy and I lived our humdrum life in suburbia.'

I remembered those years of boredom and desperation. Troy and I were never suited, he was a corporate lawyer who hunted money like it was going out of style. He wanted the beautiful wife, the beautiful house, the beautiful car and I never ticked any boxes.

The decades passed and the year I turned forty Shirley returned back to our hometown for the funeral of her parents who passed away together in a flash flood.

I waited until all the mourners left and she was by herself at the grave. 'My condolences,' I said, kissing her on the cheek. She'd aged well. Even though she was six months older than me her pale skin looked dewy and the black dress she wore hugged her willowy figure. I was self conscious about my middle-aged spread in my peach-coloured suit dress.

'And who is this?' I asked, as a little boy peered at me with her blue eyes.

'This is my son Artie.' She ruffled his brown hair.

'How old are you Artie?' I bent to ask him.

He held up a hand showing five fingers.

'That's a great age.'

'What about you and Troy? How many children do you have?'

'Oh, we were not blessed,' I said, my voice tight as I fielded the question. As the years passed and my womb never quickened with child we visited medical professionals. I'd hoped that I was the infertile one and I would be able to gracefully bow out of our marriage, ostensibly to give Troy a chance at happiness. Instead the doctor pronounced that Troy was sterile and I was now trapped in a vice, unable to leave or be painted as the heartless one.

'I'm so sorry.' Shirley reached out and held my arm.

I wilted. It had been so long since someone had touched me. Once Troy and I realised there was not going to be any progeny our already lacklustre love life petered out into banal lovemaking a few times a year.

'What about Artie's father?' I asked.

'It didn't work out. We met while I was living in the UK. A tumultuous love affair that ended messily. So it's just me and my boy.' She squeezed Artie's shoulders against her.

My heart clenched in pain seeing the love and affection between mother and son. If only I'd had that, my life might have been worth something.

'What are you going to do now?' I asked.

'We're leaving as soon as I put my parents' house on the market.'

'Then we'll have to make the most of our time together,' I said. 'I'll tell Troy that we're going for a coffee.' He'd pulled up on the pathway near us and I walked over without giving her a chance to respond. Troy looked quickly in Shirley's direction but didn't linger as he drove off.

We spent the next two weeks reminiscing as I helped her pack up her parents' house. 'I wish you didn't have to leave,' I said the day the real estate agent came to meet her to list the property. 'You're the only friend I ever had and the past two weeks have been the happiest days of my life since I lost Stephen. I'm going to miss you and Artie.' Hearing his name Artie appeared next to me. I lifted him up in my lap and hugged him tightly. He was such an affectionate little boy and holding him close healed my wounds.

Shirley looked at me and Artie with pain on her face. 'Maybe Artie should stay with you and Troy. He would have a better life with the two of you rather than my nomadic existence.'

'How can you say that?' I said, covering Artie's ears. 'You're a wonderful mother and he adores you.' I took her arm and pulled her closer so she was sitting on the edge of the armchair. 'I don't want the two of you to ever be separated. I just wish I could be a part of your lives. Promise me we'll keep in touch when you leave this time,' I asked as I looked up at her.

'You won't have to.' Shirley bent her head and leaned it on mine. 'We'll stay here. I'm not going to sell the house.'

I thought Shirley decided to stay to give Artie stability and routine. I didn't realise that the main reason she stayed was to give me a surrogate son.

'That was the happiest day of my life,' I told Shirley as I took off my glasses and wiped off the condensation from my tears. 'It was a new era of my life. I had my best friend, I became a surrogate aunt to Artie when you started working at the canning factory in administration. Even Troy and I came to a new understanding and were almost happy in our marriage.'

Years of happiness followed and we became a family. We were Uncle Troy and Aunt Shirley to Artie, always there for all his milestones. Artie slept over at our house nearly every weekend and even some weeknights as Shirley went to university and began collecting diplomas. When he was eighteen and went to university Troy and I contributed toward half his college fees and when he made his life in the city after graduating, Shirley and I continued our close friendship.

Decades passed and when I turned sixty-five, two life events ripped my life open and made me realise my whole life was a lie.

'Hello Shirley,' I said gently. Her eyes zeroed in on me and a tear rolled down her cheek. 'It's been two months since you came back.' I closed the notebook and returned it to my lap. 'I worried that you didn't want to see me again.'

'I'm sorry,' she whispered. 'I tried to make it right by telling Troy to marry you.'

'You can't replace people the way you do an old coat that has served its purpose,' I snapped viciously. 'Stephen was irreplaceable.'

I breathed in deeply and took off my glasses and put them into their case. 'It was quite a surprise to me when my husband of forty-five years confessed it wasn't the Baker boys that had killed my fiancé.'

I met her eyes. She was desperately looking for help.

Troy had been diagnosed with prostate cancer and one night after chemotherapy he'd broken down and told me what had happened the night of the Desperate and Dateless Ball. While they were driving Stephen home he started throwing up in the backseat. Shirley pulled over and helped him out of the car while Troy snored in the passenger seat. While Stephen was throwing up behind the car, she leaned down next to the driver's door and was redoing her lipstick looking at the side-view mirror. Troy snored loudly and jerked in the passenger seat, his arm accidentally knocking the parking brake. The car reversed down the incline, rolling onto Stephen and slowly crushing him to death as the wheels of the car pressed on his chest.

Shirley screamed in terror and woke Troy who was befuddled and drunk. Troy stumbled to the back and shouted at Shirley to move the car, while he kneeled next to Stephen who was wheezing and fighting for breath. Shirley jumped into the passenger seat and turned on the car, pressing on the pedal, and she reversed with both front and back wheels going over Stephen.

'It sounded awful,' Shirley cried. 'The way he fought to breath as he died. He kept calling your name.'

My hands fisted into my lap, the arthritis gnawing at my knuckles. I hated this part, when she attempted justifying her actions.

'Yes, and you had your whole life ahead of you and a jail sentence for manslaughter would have jeopardised it,' I said, repeating Troy's reasoning for why they had covered up Stephen's murder by taking his dead body to his parents' farm and leaving it at the top of the driveway.

'But no more awful than finding out my whole life was a lie.'

When Troy passed away I found the letters they exchanged after we married. That had been the worst of it. I knew that marrying Troy was a mistake from the moment I stepped out of the church. Beside him I looked awkward and plain. I never fit into his world and always felt like I'd been trying to live up to Shirley. When I read their letters I found out they'd still desperately loved each other, but that it had been Shirley's way of trying to atone for what she did to Stephen by getting Troy to marry me.

'It's okay, Shirley. I forgive you.' I patted her hand. 'After all you have suffered too. Remember Artie?

Her face brightened at the mention of her son. 'Is he coming to visit?'

'Artie is dead,' I told her. 'Don't you remember? You hit him with your car. You crushed him under the front wheels.'

I watched the pain on her face as the memory of Stephen's death merged with the image of Artie.

'No, no,' she screamed, covering her face. 'I killed my son. I killed my son.'

'It's alright Shirley. It was an accident.' I hugged her. After all my years of mourning the children I could never have, I knew that Shirley's pain at the death of her child by her own hand would be the most gruesome revenge I could inflict on her. I suspected that even when she was lost in the haze of her dementia, she was haunted by the spectre of her culpability.

Her eyes returned to their frozen stare of horror.

I sighed. Her stays were becoming shorter and shorter. I gasped as the pain cut through me and pressed the buzzer. Anne came and helped me to bed. 'I'm going to bring your pain medication,' she said.

I didn't argue. The pain was too strong. The cancer was spreading and I didn't have much time left. I looked into Shirley's blank stare. Still there should be enough time for one more visit, one more hit to make up for the lifetime of treason, and then I would be done.

Anne returned and I took the medication she held out. Lethargy gripped me as the pain medication did its job. After Anne left I picked up the notebook and flipped to the back cover. I unpeeled it from the backing and lifted out the photo.

It was the night of the Desperate and Dateless Ball and the four of us were smiling in the camera, our arms looped around each other so we were like one entity.

'Shirley, do you remember how we said we'd be friends forever?'

It had been after Stephen had died. I'd been crying in her arms and she'd cried with me.

'I'll always be here,' she'd said. 'We'll be friends forever.'

'You were right, Shirley,' I told her. 'We'll always be together. I've arranged for us to be buried side-by-side.'

My eyes closed as the drug took me under.

School of Hardknocks

The students carried the boy spread-eagled and slammed his genitals against a pole. He dropped on the concrete like a sack of potatoes, holding his crotch, squirming in pain. Sounds that I didn't think a human could produce came out of his throat.

'Bastard just got knackered.' Kayla laughed, noticing my horror. 'Every school tour starts like this.'

Kayla was my new schoolmate and she was giving me a tour of my new school, The Tech, under orders from our Year 7 homeroom teacher. Her friend Sharon was tagging along and she sniggered too.

Feeling nauseous, I wondered what I would see next as we continued around the school grounds.

'He'll be walking like a cowboy tomorrow,' Sharon said beside us, shaking her brown curly hair. My eyes caught on her Barbra Streisand honker, and it was only when I really focused on her other features that I noticed she had pretty hazel eyes and a full mouth.

'Don't ever wear tracksuit pants to school.' Kayla was the archetypal Anglo girl, tall and skinny, with white blonde hair and freckles.

'Why?' My new school had a uniform and Mum had bought me tracksuit pants with it.

'Because you'll get *dacked*,' Sharon said. 'They pull down your trackies and expose your underwear for everyone to see.'

'Or if you wear tracksuit pants, at least wear pretty undies.' Kayla pulled up her dress and showed me her striped blue and white underpants with a white bow in front.

I looked away from Kayla's underwear, feeling my cheeks go hot. While I blended into the very Anglo school with my blonde hair and green eyes, I had an accent. I spoke Bosnian as my first language for four years of my life and always over-corrected my vowels. People often asked me if I was British or South African. My accent proclaimed me an exotic species and I was a hot commodity — the new girl who had arrived in the middle of the school term. Kayla and Sharon had an apostle.

'Oh my God, she's blushing.' Sharon peered at my face.

'She's so cute.' Kayla put her hand through mine.

'Like a little puppy,' Sharon said.

'You'll have to toughen up, Amina,' Kayla said. 'The Tech is not for the faint-hearted.'

The Tech was not our first choice of school. My mother had taken my brother and I back to Bosnia for a holiday that became a four-year stay. When we returned to St Albans, a suburb in the western suburbs of Melbourne, I was twelve years old. My mother tried to enrol me in the high school on the other side of the train tracks — it was perceived as the good high school because the punch-ups took place off school grounds in the nearby park — but we were told there were no openings. The teachers there suggested that I enrol in grade six and then start year seven the year after. But I refused to go backwards. The education system in Bosnia was much more rigorous and I knew I'd have no trouble keeping up, so Mum enroled me in a school that was closer to home.

The school was named after the street it faced, but no one ever called it that. Instead they called it *The Tech* after its previous incarnation as a technical college for boys. Most of the classes were orientated toward the trades: sheet metal, woodwork, auto workshop. Then, along with the new female cohort, other subjects were added: typing, home economics and sewing.

There were punch-ons nearly every week, some on the grounds and some after school in the adjoining streets and park. Even teachers weren't immune to being clocked on the job by a belligerent student. Teachers survived by developing a thick skin and ingenious classroom management. Our woodwork teacher got our attention by taking out his glass eye and placing it on the desk. 'I'm keeping an eye on you,' he'd say, to the delight of the kids.

A few days later after I started at The Tech we were in the toilets during recess. 'Shit, I got my rags,' Kayla said from inside the cubicle.

'What are rags?' I asked Sharon who was standing next to me, looking at herself in the mirror.

'Period,' Sharon said. She was used to my naivety and constant questions as I adapted to being in Australia once again.

'I need a tampon,' Kayla called out.

Sharon reached into her backpack and took out a slim, white capsule, passing it to Kayla under the cubicle door. 'You don't know what a tampon is?' Sharon asked, seeing my face.

I shook my head. I didn't even really know what a period was. I had gone to Bosnia as an eight-year-old and had lived with my grandparents for four years while my mother was in and out of hospital. My grandparents were old-fashioned and had sheltered me from adult matters — whenever there was a kissing scene on TV my brother and I had been sent out of the living room to wait in the hallway until it was safe to return. Now I was thrust into the rough and tumble world of adolescence and I was not well prepared.

'You put a tampon inside to collect the blood.' Sharon mimed the insertion of a tampon.

I did my best not to audibly gulp. That sounded incredibly painful. A few minutes later, Kayla came out of the toilet and washed her hands. We walked out of the toilets and down the corridor. We passed by the Year 9 locker bays and a boy turned and smiled at me. I'd noticed him smiling my way a few times before and I always smiled back.

'I think Jeremy likes you,' Kayla said as she noticed our exchange.

Sharon turned to look over her shoulder. 'He's still looking.'

'Do you like him?' Kayla asked.

Even though my body had started blooming — three pubic hairs had sprouted and my breast tissue was tender — I was still unsure if I wanted a boyfriend, and even if I did, Jeremy would not have been a contender. He had brown hair and nondescript features. He wasn't the sort of boy that girls noticed.

'I don't—'

'I'll bet he wants you to be his girlfriend.' Kayla cut me off before I could finish saying that I didn't know if I liked him. We'd never spoken and our only contact had been a few smiles in passing.

'Wouldn't that be great,' Sharon said.

'But I don't know anything about him,' I said.

'He's in year nine and everyone knows him,' Kayla said.

'Did you have a boyfriend before?' Sharon asked.

I shook my head. I had only developed my first crush in the three months before I left Bosnia for Australia. His name was Samir and he was the smartest boy in my class. All we did was exchange glances and smiles, and when I stopped studying because I knew I was returning to Australia, and couldn't answer the teacher's questions, he moved from the front row to sit beside me in the back and whispered the answers.

'Have you ever kissed a boy?' Sharon asked.

I shook my head again.

'We'll have to fix that,' Kayla said.

I looked at her wide smile with trepidation. I had been shocked to find out that Kayla had kissed her first boy in fifth grade and had already had a few boyfriends, while Sharon had had her first kiss when she was in grade six. Sharon and her boyfriend broke up when they went to different high schools and now she was on the lookout for her first high school boyfriend. In Bosnia, old fashioned attitudes and expectations about female virtue prevailed. A girl was supposed to avoid members of the opposite sex in case she got a bad reputation. I had once returned home from a female friend's house and my grandfather had beat my fingertips with a stick — I could only imagine the punishment he would have meted out for kissing a boy.

That night I went home and searched through the bathroom medicine cabinet until I found Mum's box of tampons. I took one out of the packet and retreated to my room. After locking my door I sat on the bed and took the plastic sheath off the little white capsule. The tampon was smooth and I spent some time tugging on the string at the bottom until I figured out its purpose. After taking off my undies, I spread my legs, held the tampon against my vagina and pushed it in. It felt dry and slightly uncomfortable, but I persisted until my finger and the tampon were in all the way.

I got up and walked around. I couldn't really feel it inside, but the string was annoying as it tickled my thighs. I sat back on the bed and tugged the string to remove the tampon and winced and moaned as the dry tampon chaffed against my insides. After I'd tugged it out, I held my hand against my crotch until the pain subsided. When I got it out, the tampon was slightly swollen, but otherwise looked much the same. I vowed never to use a tampon again.

The next day Kayla and Sharon greeted me at the school gates with beaming smiles. They told me that Jeremy liked me and wanted to ask me out. 'So we told him that you like him too. You do like him, don't you?' Sharon asked, noticing my shock.

'Of course she does,' Kayla interrupted. 'She was smiling at him.'

The two of them stared at me as they waited for an answer. I wanted to tell them that I didn't want a boyfriend, but I had already noticed the hierarchy in our little threesome: Kayla was the leader, Sharon her little follower, and I was expected to be the yes girl who went along with whatever they wanted. I nodded. Maybe it wouldn't be too bad; besides which, it was kind of nice to know that a boy liked me, even though I didn't like him back.

At lunchtime, we gathered in the school courtyard. I was on one side with my girlfriends, he was on the other with his mates. His best friend, Caine, walked over. 'Jeremy wants to know if you will go out with him,' he said.

I nodded.

Kayla, answered for me, 'Yes, she will.'

Caine returned back to Jeremy and gave him my answer. Jeremy smiled and we were nudged together, while our friends formed a crowd and watched. We exchanged awkward conversation. He put his hand around my waist and we acted the part of the happy couple. I'd never been this close to a boy and I didn't know how to stand, or what to say. Soon enough he retreated back to his mates, and I went back to Kayla and Sharon.

'What did you talk about?' Kayla demanded when I returned.

'He asked where I had moved from.' It was slightly ludicrous that I now had a boyfriend who didn't know the first thing about me.

'You know what happens now,' Sharon said. 'Now you have to get on.'

'What's *get on*?' I asked, feeling my heart race in panic. Did that mean he had to get on me? Did that mean we had to have sex?

'That's what we call kissing,' Kayla said.

My panic subsided, but I was still feeling trepidation. Why was kissing called *getting on*? Was it regular kissing or was there more to it?

I was going through a growth spurt and ate multiple times a day, so at recess the next day I bought my favourite meal: a hamburger and chocolate milkshake and wolfed it down.

'Yuck,' Kayla said. 'You're going to have hamburger breath when you kiss.'

I hadn't even thought about the mechanics of my new status or the expectations on me. The food I'd just eaten curdled in my stomach.

At lunchtime, Jeremy found me and we walked hand in hand to the oval, our friends walking behind us. Jeremy took me to the edge of the oval and we stood behind a bush. As Jeremy put his hands on my waist and bent to kiss me I heard our friends on the other side of the bush laughing and talking as they maintained our faux-privacy. I was in a ditch and he was taller than he usually was so I had to stand on tippy toes. As we began kissing, I took my cue from him and opened my mouth and joined it to his. Jeremy's mouth was minty fresh. My friends told me later that he kept a toothbrush and toothpaste in his locker. We imitated a fish's mouth as we mashed our lips together. Every few minutes he tilted his head to the other side and I followed suit by tilting mine in the opposite direction so our noses didn't smack each other's.

After a few minutes I opened my eyes and watched him. He had his eyes firmly closed as he sucked at my mouth. We kissed for so long that my calf began aching and cramping, but at least the discomfort was keeping the boredom at bay.

Kayla walked around the bush and interrupted us. 'Fourteen minutes,' she said, tapping her watch.

Jeremy smiled, satisfied that he'd achieved his personal best. He took my hand and we joined our friends. I felt like I had a clown mouth, our co-mingled saliva coating my cheeks and chin. I surreptitiously lifted my hand and wiped the drool with my sleeve.

'You can't do that,' his best friend Caine said when he spotted me doing it. 'You can't wipe someone's kiss off you.'

I turned red with embarrassment and looked at the ground.

'It's okay.' Jeremy hugged me tight.

'How was the kiss?' Sharon quizzed me the next day.

'Wet,' I said.

She and Kayla exchanged a look.

'What do you mean?' Kayla asked.

'My mouth was all wet.' I touched the skin around my mouth and chin.

'I thought he'd be a good kisser because he's had lots of girl-friends,' Kayla said.

'You mean it's not supposed to be like that?' I asked in surprise.

'No.' Sharon shook her head. 'I loved kissing my boyfriend.' She sighed as she stared into space.

'Do you want me to dump him for you?' Kayla asked.

'Really?' I was surprised she was so eager considering she'd been so quick to matchmake.

'Sure. I'm sure your next boyfriend will be a much better kisser.'

True to her word, Kayla went to speak to Jeremy's best friend and gave him the news. The next time I saw Jeremy in the corridor I wanted to run in the other direction, but he smiled and waved at me, letting me know he harbored no ill will. My short-lived romance left me with no negative after-effects, apart from a distaste of kissing.

Jeremy didn't pine for long. Within a fortnight, he'd hooked up with another candidate and this girlfriend stuck around for a while. I developed a new method of repelling unwanted male attention by developing a crush on the most unattainable boy in our high school.

Over time everything settled back to normal, except for my friendship with Kayla and Sharon. Their viciousness was seeping through and since I was the lowest in the pecking order, I was always the one who had to act on their dares and was the butt of their jokes.

A few months later I walked over to Katherine, a girl I considered my friend. Katherine looked at me, waiting for me to speak. I hesitated, not wanting to follow through on the dare to kick Katherine. I glanced over at Kayla and Sharon. Kayla was staring me down, while Sharon looked away.

My leg seemed to move of its own volition and I kicked Katherine in the shin. Katherine's face tightened. I saw betrayal in her eyes. I wanted to apologise and beg for forgiveness, but I knew not to show weakness.

Katherine braced herself on the wall. She lifted her leg back and kicked me back, her chunky black shoe leaving dark marks on my shins. I knew in that moment that I had transgressed. We were both victims of bullying and Katherine was easy fodder. She was pretty, even though pimples covered her face, the white pus oozing out and looking like semen so that she was often taunted with comments like, 'don't you wash your face after getting cum on it?' While Katherine, like me, had to take her licks when they came, she wasn't going to take them from *me*.

Behind me, Sharon and Kayla were giggling, finding my whole performance hysterical. As I slinked back, my shins throbbing and my eyes tearing from humiliation and pain, Kayla shrieked with high-pitched laughter.

'I can't believe she kicked you back,' Kayla said.

'And you took it like a chump.' Sharon clutched her stomach as she laughed.

Later that month, Kayla had a birthday party and I felt the familiar spin cycle of trepidation and excitement in my stomach at the thought of spending a night with my friends. I had never participated in a sleepover and the only reason I could go was because Mum was in hospital and unaware of my plans, and my stepfather had given permission to end my pleading.

When I arrived, the house was full with all of Kayla's friends already in attendance. We spent the night talking, watching movies and eating snacks. Eventually we exhausted ourselves and fell asleep in the early morning.

I woke sometime during the night to a tingly, cold sensation on my skin. I touched my arm and felt something sticky and shrieked with panic. I heard giggles in the dark.

'Shhh, you'll wake my parents,' Kayla said.

There was a click and the lamp beside her bed came on. I blinked my eyes in the bright light and saw that the girls were sitting around me. Kayla held a toothpaste tube in her hand and I looked down and saw the smeared blue streak of it on my arm. I started crying, caught off guard in the state between wakefulness and sleep, impotent rage and sadness filling me.

'Don't be a cry baby,' Kayla said. 'It's just a prank.'

I saw the disgust and embarrassment on the faces of my friends. I had violated our friendship by not being a good sport. 'I'm not crying because of that,' I lied. 'I was dreaming about my dad and it made me cry.'

Like most female friendships, our connection was predicated on the age-old rituals of secret telling. Soon after becoming friends, I'd confessed to Sharon and Kayla my life story, including my father's death and my mother's medical condition. I had also earned my popularity because I was able to bring friends home during school lunch breaks when Mum was in hospital and my stepfather was visiting her. My friends asked for coffee.

The only coffee my parents drank was Minas freshly roasted coffee that my stepfather ground using a hand grinder. I made them coffee in the traditional Bosnian fashion by spooning six teaspoons in a *džezva*, Bosnian coffee pot, on the stove and served it on a tray with *fildžani*, small demitasse cups. I demonstrated how they needed to drink the coffee by breaking off some of the square sugar cube and placing it in my mouth and then sipping the coffee. Sharon and Kayla followed suit, scrunching up their faces as they tasted the bitterness of the coffee. After that I served English breakfast tea only.

I had learnt to bridge the gap between us by concealing my differences and so now as I pretended to cry because of a dream about my father, I felt relief as Sharon hugged me.

'Poor thing,' Sharon said over my shoulder.

I saw Kayla's sour face before hiding my face in Sharon's hair. Sharon took me to the bathroom where I washed my arm and face. I returned to Kayla's bedroom where all the girls rallied around me, and fell asleep feeling comforted and loved.

The next morning we went to a swimming pool. I watched in envy as my girlfriends donned bikinis that emphasised their curvy bodies, while I put on my red and black one-piece suit. We followed Kayla out to the swimming pool and arranged our towels and bags on the green grass beside the pool. We didn't worry about sunscreen and none of us had brought any, although Kayla had brought a zinc tube that she used to draw patterns on our body so that we would have tan line shapes after the day. She drew a smiley face on her stomach, a big heart on Sharon's back, and a star on my thigh.

'All right, let's go in.' She ran toward the edge of the pool, leaping into the air and holding her knees to her chest as she hit the water.

The rest of my friends followed suit, while I gingerly walked to the ladder and slowly submerged myself. Kayla and the girls kept swimming into the deep end, while I clung to the edge. I had learnt to swim as a child and could keep afloat comfortably, but I'd had a scare a few months ago when I'd gone to the sea with a family friend. I'd walked into the water, enjoying the feeling of the squishy sand in my toes, and had stepped into a depression, the water suddenly reaching my neck. As I tried to take a step back to safety I'd lost my footing. A wave crashed over my head and I went under, struggling to scramble back to the surface. As I flailed in panic I swallowed water, and the coughing fit sent me back under. I could see the sky above me, but I kept sinking, my hands reaching for something to hold, but there was nothing.

Suddenly arms reached for me and the husband of my family friend carried me out, where I coughed up the water, my throat feeling scratchy and sore. I didn't risk going in past my knees for the rest of the day, and now that I was in the swimming pool I wasn't going to risk going in any further than my waist.

Sharon came to keep me company and we leant our backs against the side of the pool as we talked.

'What are you doing over there?' Kayla demanded, as she swam over from the deep end.

'Nothing,' I said.

'Come here.'

Sharon went to her, and I took a step toward them, but as soon as the water pressure hit my chest and I struggled to breathe, the familiar panic took hold and I returned to the shallow end.

Annoyance spread over Kayla's face when I didn't obey her command. She smiled and called our friends toward her. I felt a portent of danger and quickly climbed up the ladder and out of the pool. I was lying on my towel, pretending I wanted to get a suntan when they all came and stood around me.

'Let's go.' Kayla grabbed hold of my arms.

The other girls grabbed my other limbs and tried to carry me to the pool.

'No, stop,' I begged. 'Please, don't.'

'Stop being a baby,' Kayla shouted, her face red from the exertion of carrying me.

As I caught sight of the pool edge I fought like a cornered animal, kicking and pushing them away until they let go. The girls watched me with anger. Sharon rubbed her leg where I'd kicked her and Kayla looked down at the drops of blood on her arm where I'd scratched her.

Kayla shoved her face into mine. 'Why are you being such a spoilsport?'

I was mute, unable to speak from terror. Kayla slapped me on the face, the sound of her palm hitting my cheek with a loud smack. One of the girls giggled from behind us. 'Fuck off, you dumb bitch,' Kayla hissed.

I grabbed my towel and bag of clothes, running to the pay phone next to the change rooms where I called my stepfather to pick me up. He drove me to Kayla's house where her mother let me into the house to collect my belongings.

'What happened?' he asked as he drove me home.

'Nothing. I just got sunburnt,' I lied.

By the end of the year I was worn out by the relentless bullying. At my urging, my parents enroled me in the school on the other side of the train tracks.

I saw Sharon only once after I changed schools. We passed each other as we walked in opposite directions on Main Road after school. She made eye contact, by accident, and then quickly looked away. I was relegated to someone she used to know. I walked on, my head high and my back straight.

Woman on Fire

It began two months ago when my mother took me to visit Muamer for the first time. He lived in Footscray, in a narrow street built for horse-drawn carriages. His house was a white weatherboard with a tin roof and wraparound porch. After we arrived he led me back out the front door.

'Over there's a park,' he said, and pointed down the street. 'You go there and play.'

I sullenly walked to the park. I was seven; old enough to understand why I was sent away.

When I returned, Mum and Muamer were not in the living room where I'd left them. I ran through the hallway in panic. Hearing them talk from a closed bedroom door I pushed it open. Muamer was standing beside the bed in a dark blue silk robe that shimmered over his potbelly. The short robe barely grazed his thighs; his hairy legs stuck out of the bottom of the robe. He looked embarrassed when I walked in. Mum didn't move from where she lay. Muamer picked something up from the bed and headed for the door.

'What's that in your hand?' I demanded, my eyes caught by the stealthy way he crumpled the cloth.

'My socks.' His face turned red. It was his underwear, black cotton briefs. After he left, Mum looked at me.

'Get out,' she said, her green eyes glowing. As I closed the door I saw her stand up, her pale-fleshed body nude. It wasn't the first time I'd caught her in bed with a man.

Soon, life became unpredictable and strange. Mum met Muamer on the rebound and leaped into an ill-fated relationship. Muamer was not her type or age appropriate. She never found out his age because he'd scratched out his date of birth on his driver's licence. Mum was twenty-nine and exercised every day to maintain her figure. Muamer was possessive and there were daily fights. Soon he found that he could use his strength to control her.

Muamer's house was old, and had no inside toilet; instead there was an outhouse in the small, concrete enclosed backyard. At night I was too scared to go out. Mum's solution was for me to pee into a bucket that she flushed the next day. Each morning I stared into the bucket, my urine a dark yellow mixture with bits of toilet paper weighing it down, the strong smell wafting up my nostrils.

I was waiting for breakfast while Muamer and Mum shouted. They'd been arguing all morning. Muamer pursued her
doggedly around the house, accusing her of flirting with some
man or another as she tried to make breakfast. Mum tried to go
to the kitchen, but he grabbed her by the arms and wrenched
her back.

'You are my everything.' His voice was full of pain. I watched
from the doorway in my pyjamas as Mum pulled away from
him.

'Just tell me you love me,' he pleaded. He grabbed her again
but she managed to throw him off. She picked up the pee bucket
and tossed it at him. Urine soaked his hair and chest, bits of
toilet paper stuck to his cheeks and shoulder.

'Run.' She yanked me down the hallway and out the front
door.

We ran down the street to the house of a Bosnian family we
knew. I kept looking behind us to see if Muamer was following,
but he was nowhere to be seen. Mum told the neighbours about
the fight, her voice loud as she barely stopped for pause. Her
tongue got thick, her speech slurred. The neighbours exchanged
looks of concern as they listened to her. They gave me toast to
eat and sent me to the living room to watch television while they
remained in the kitchen talking to Mum.

Eventually, there was a knock on the door. The woman of the house answered, leading in Muamer. He looked sheepish, his hair wet.

'He keeps following me,' Mum shrieked. 'He thinks I'm having an affair.'

'Now, now, calm down, Senka.' Muamer's calm voice was a stark contrast to Mum's accusations. 'There's nothing to be upset about.'

'You never leave me alone,' she shouted. 'I have no peace from you, accusing me of cheating, calling me a slut!'

I snuck to the doorway and saw Mum bunched up against the wall. He was reaching his arms out to her, like she was a wild animal that needed to be contained. The Bosnian couple watched the spectacle.

'Ask Elma.' Mum pointed at me. 'Ask her how he torments me.'

The wife was moved from her inertia and quickly ran over to me, tugging me away.

'Mummy,' I called out and began crying. 'I want Mummy.'

I tried to push the woman away, but she held onto me as Muamer and her husband led Mum out of the house.

Mum was admitted into hospital. After a few weeks of heavy sedation and occasional visits, Mum stabilised and progressed to weekend visits. On Friday night Muamer picked her up from the hospital, and on Monday morning, he would drive her back.

I was used to fending for myself. Mum had frequent mental breakdowns as a lifelong Bipolar sufferer, and I'd ended up being cared for by various family friends across the years. With Mum becoming a weekend parent, I settled into a new life during the weekdays. The playground became my second home and I played there after school until it was night. I made friends with other feral neighbourhood children.

It was during this time that I met Lucy. Lucy lived a few streets away, but had found her way to our park and it became her daily haunt. She was about my age and we grew close quickly, as children do.

Lucy was always reluctant to go home. I stayed out all afternoon, but still when darkness stretched across the playground, Muamer shouted my name from the front porch. While home wasn't a joyful place, it also wasn't a place I dreaded. Many nights when I walked toward the shining light on the porch I looked over my shoulder and saw Lucy on the swing, her face etched in sadness as she delayed going home. Muamer didn't allow any kids to visit. My friendships took place in the park and nowhere else.

One weeknight when I finished playing and just before Muamer came to call me, Lucy asked me if I wanted to sleep over at her house. I'd never had a sleepover at anyone's house and this seemed the most exciting thing that could possibly happen.

We ran together to Muamer's house. I yanked open the door and yelled out asking permission to sleep over. I'm not sure why he said yes. Perhaps he didn't understand the concept of a sleepover, or maybe he thought I was asking to visit. It didn't occur to me to pack anything, such as a change of clothes or a toothbrush. We flew off the porch and ran into the darkened streets. Lucy didn't live far, just a few winding streets down. When we got to her house her mother had visitors so we retreated to her bedroom.

Her house had threadbare carpets and the walls were flaking. I didn't get the chance to visit many other girls' bedrooms and was intensely curious. Lucy's bedroom was used as a storage area for her mother's things, and there was barely enough room from the bed to the door to walk. On the floor were clothes and she didn't have many toys.

Quickly, the house filled with adults. Music was turned up loud, and the smell of cigarettes permeated the house. At some point we left the room to eat and entered the crowded living room.

'There's my girl,' her mum drawled, holding a beer in one hand and cigarette in the other. Lucy made her way through the bodies that were seated on the floor and every available piece of furniture until we reached the couch where her mother sat.

Her boyfriend was beside her. He scooped Lucy up and put her on his lap and tickled her. Lucy didn't look happy, but she didn't get up. After a few minutes of enduring the conversation around us, Lucy stood and took me to the kitchen where we made ourselves a sandwich from stale bread.

We returned to her bedroom and ate, and then got ready for sleep.

'You have to take off your underwear,' Lucy said, slipping off her panties under the doona and throwing them on the floor.

'Why?' I asked, finding this strange.

'You just do,' Lucy said and closed her eyes.

Lucy fast fell asleep, untroubled by the sounds of shrieking conversations as drunk and stoned friends of her mother fought to be heard over the throbbing music. As I lay beside her, the unfamiliar feeling of bed sheets tickling my private parts, I couldn't settle as I processed all the strange things I'd seen and heard. Eventually exhaustion dragged me under.

When we awoke the house was deserted, with remnants of the party strewn all over the living room. Lucy warned me to keep quiet, as her mother would be in a bad mood after a hard night. We had a silent breakfast and left the house.

As we walked to the town centre Lucy pointed out a house with garden beds neatly planted with plastic tulips in colourful rows.

'Let's get one,' Lucy dared. I looked back at the house. Something about the way the plastic flowers were symmetrically rising out of the garden bed touched my heart. There was a beauty in this display and I wondered at the person who arranged this. Seeing Lucy's wicked smile I realised she didn't feel this sentiment and so I nodded. We jumped over the fence and each grabbed a fake tulip and ran as we laughed fiendishly. When we reached the end of the street Lucy threw her plastic flower on the grass. I hesitated before following suit, remembering the empty space in the flowerbed.

We spent the day window-shopping. At some point we ended up in a toy shop and I looked at all the toys I didn't have with envy twisting inside me. I picked up a Cabbage Patch doll and gently caressed her chubby, plastic cheek.

'Do you want it?' Lucy asked.

'Yeah, but Mum can't afford it,' I said, regretfully returning it to the shelf. Cabbage Patch dolls were expensive and I'd coveted one ever since I saw the first commercial on television.

'Who said you needed your mum?' Lucy asked scornfully. She looked craftily around us. 'Get ready to run,' she whispered. She grabbed the doll and ran to the door. I hesitated for a split second, shocked at her cunning. Realising I was an accessory, my survival instinct kicked in. We ran until we were again in the quiet streets of suburbia.

Lucy eventually stopped. I caught up to her and we were both bent forward as we fought to get our breath back.

'Here,' she said, a big smile on her face. I took the doll gingerly. I'd dreamed about the moment when I would finally have my own Cabbage Patch doll for so long, yet now that I finally held one in my arms, it felt tainted.

We spent a few more hours out and about and when dark approached Lucy asked me again to sleepover at her house.

'I'll have to ask Muamer,' I said cautiously.

'No need,' Lucy said. 'If he said okay once already, he wouldn't have a problem with another night.'

This logic seemed to make sense and so I agreed.

'We can't take the doll home, though,' Lucy said.

'Why?' I asked, hugging it tighter.

'Mum will want to know where I got it.'

Something in her face made me not ask questions. I left the doll on a bench and as dark descended we walked to her house. This time it was quiet with no party, however her mum and boyfriend were in the living room wrapped around each other. We went to bed, again removing our underwear, and slept.

In the morning I awoke with my stomach twisting with hunger. I hadn't eaten much the day before and was feeling it.

We went to the kitchen, but there was no bread, no milk, no cereal.

Lucy's mum came in, her face wan.

'Mum, can you give me money to buy something to eat?' Lucy asked.

'Shut the fuck up!' Her mum exploded into rage. She picked Lucy up and threw her against the wall.

My body burst into motion before my mind had time to process the action. I ran all the way home to Muamer's house, not looking back once. When I got home Muamer told me he looked for me the night before, driving up and down the dark streets of Footscray. He was too relieved that I was back to scold me.

In hospital Mum was seeing a female Muslim psychiatrist. They bonded on the basis of their shared religion, and she was the one who truly triggered a change in Mum. She was shocked by the weekend parenting arrangement.

'What do you think you're doing?' she demanded when Mum explained that Muamer, a man she barely knew, was caring for me. 'You keep this up and your child will be taken from you.'

These words woke Mum up. She'd once told me that being in hospital was like a vacation for her. Being a sole parent was a heavy burden for her to carry, but when the psychiatrist made her realise what she was risking, she sought release from hospital and came home. To celebrate, she and Muamer planned a family camping trip.

The wind rustling through the trees and the cacophony of bird-calls woke me. I opened my eyes and saw the emerald colour of the nylon tent roof. Through it I could picture the tree branches that we slept beneath twirling in the wind, producing nature's symphony. I lifted my head and on the other side of the tent lay my mum and Muamer.

Feeling the press of my bladder I reluctantly unzipped the sleeping bag and slid out, like a critter being born. When I pushed open the tent door a panoramic view of greenery greeted me. We had pitched our tent on a clearing surrounded by bushes and trees. As I walked straight ahead to the trees I heard the river rushing past behind the foliage.

A few metres from us was another tent for Behija and Eldin and their two sons. Behija was Mum's best friend. Behija and Eldin used to be tobacco share crop farmers in Myrtleford and Mum had met them when she lived on a farm with her first husband. They'd invited us on this camping trip, their annual family holiday. Muamer wasn't happy with the fact that Behija and Eldin had a claim on Mum's affections. He wanted her isolated and vulnerable, and surrounded by friends. She was beginning to show strength.

That night, Eldin and his sons built a fire in the pit they had created away from the tents. We gathered around, adults sitting on foldaway chairs, while the rest of us sat on logs. Marshmallows, sticks and fire were ready. As we talked, Muamer sipped *rakija,* a Balkan plum brandy from the bottle he kept at his feet. It didn't take long for the alcohol to fan the flames of his paranoia, and he started making accusations about Mum's chastity. He couldn't believe that my beautiful mother had chosen him and was always on the lookout for betrayal. Her white unmarked skin and thin waistline were a stark contrast to his short tubby body, greying hair and the alcohol-broken-capillaries on his nose and cheeks. A smile exchanged with a male acquaintance or an innocent glance at a shopkeeper became events worthy of an inquisition.

'Where were you?' he demanded. 'You were with someone. Who is he?'

Eldin and Behija tried to intervene, but he pushed Eldin away. They retreated, shocked by this violent outburst, probably fearing for their sons' safety, and I'm sure feeling some anger at Mum for putting them in this position and tainting their family holiday.

Mum tried to move away from Muamer, but he grabbed hold of her, trying to restrain her. They wrestled, moving closer to the fire, when he pushed her. Her arms flailed as she fought to catch her balance. The fire behind her rose bigger and brighter, lighting up her frightened face. A scream trapped in my throat as I watched her fall.

Eldin rushed forward and pushed Muamer back. They argued while I wrapped myself around Mum's shivering thighs. A few minutes later Muamer drove off in a rage, tyres throwing up earth and gravel as he sped off.

He stayed away that night and came back the next morning. We packed up our tent and went home with him. Mum had a lot of time to think on the trip back. Muamer pulled up in the driveway of his house and got out of the car to open the gate, leaving the engine running. While he unlocked the gate, Mum jumped over the gear stick and sat in the driver's seat. She threw the car in reverse and burst onto the street, the car veering as she sped away from Muamer.

We had nowhere to go, so like a swallow in spring, Mum returned to the only home we'd ever had, the house my father bought and renovated, and that his death insurance had paid for. It was being rented by a distant female cousin on my father's side. The woman greeted us at the gate. We stood like beggars speaking to her through the bars. In the end she agreed to give us shelter and the gate squeaked as she opened it and let us inside.

We pitched the tent under the branches of a mulberry tree I climbed throughout my childhood. We lay in the tent, the nylon shushing from the wind, as the branches above us rustled in the wind. I curled against Mum's side.

'It's my birthday tomorrow,' Mum said, tears in her voice.

'I'll buy you a cake,' I said.

'Thank you my baby.'

I fell asleep, but my slumber was disturbed by tremors. I forced my eyelids open.

Mum was crying silently, her chest heaving as she held in her sobs. I fell asleep again while the wind witnessed Mum's silent tears. It was her thirtieth birthday.

I snuck out before she awoke. I'd slept in my clothes. Mum's purse was on the tent floor. I opened it and took out two gold coins. I walked two blocks to the milk bar where I picked out a birthday card and roulade cake. When I got back Mum was still sleeping.

'Happy birthday to you,' I sang softly. Mum sat up in the sleeping bag, her hair dishevelled, her face creased from the pillow.

'Happy birthday, Mummy,' I said, handing over the card and the cake. I didn't have a pen, and the card was blank.

'Thank you,' Mum said, hugging me and kissing my head. Her tears dried in my hair.

About the Author

Amra Pajalić is an award-winning author, an editor and teacher who draws on her Bosnian cultural heritage to write own voices stories for young people, who like her, are searching to mediate their identity and take pride in their diverse culture.

She won the 2009 Melbourne Prize for Literature's Civic Choice Award for her debut novel *The Good Daughter*. The anthology she co-edited, *Growing up Muslim in Australia* (Allen and Unwin, 2014), was shortlisted for the 2015 Children's Book Council of the year awards and her memoir *Things Nobody Knows But Me* (Transit Lounge, 2019) was shortlisted for the 2020 National Biography Award. Her short stories and non-fiction articles and essays have been been published in anthologies, journals and shortlisted in writing competitions. She works as a high school teacher and is completing a PhD in Creative Writing at La Trobe University.

CONNECT WITH AMRA:

www.amrapajalic.com

https://www.instagram.com/amrapajalicauthor/

https://twitter.com/AmraPajalic

https://www.tiktok.com/@amrapajalic

https://www.facebook.com/AmraPajalicAuthor/

https://www.bookbub.com/authors/amra-pajalic

SIGN UP FOR AMRA'S AUTHOR NEWSLETTER

For news, giveaways, bonus material, and sneak peeks, please sign up to her newsletter.

http://www.amrapajalic.com/

PLEASE LEAVE A REVIEW

If you enjoyed this book and would like to show Amra your support, please consider leaving a star rating and/or review on the website you purchased the book from or on Amra's Goodreads page or Amazon Author Central page.

Short Story Publication Credits

Amra's stories were previously published in online journals, anthologies and shortlisted in prizes:

'The Cuckoo's Song', Second Prize, 2006 *Brimbank Council Short Story Competition*

'Siege' published in 2004 *Best Australian Short Stories*, Black Inc

'Flirty Eyes' in 2005 *Best Australian Short Stories*, Black Inc

'In Treatment' published in the 2011 *Ada Cambridge* Competition Anthology

'Fragments' published in *Bronzeville Bee* Online Journal, 2019

'Nervous Breakdown' previously published in 2016 *Rebellious Daughters* Anthology, Ventura Press

'School of Hard Knocks' in *Meet me at the Intersection* anthology, Freemantle Press, 2018

'Woman on Fire' in 2013 *Etchings* journal

A guide for international readers

This book is set in Australia and uses British English spelling. Some spellings may differ from those used in American English.

Australia's seasons are at opposite times to those in the northern hemisphere. Summer is December–February, autumn is March–May, winter is June–August, and spring is September–November. Christmas is in summer.

In the Australian school system, primary school is for grades Kindergarten to Grade 6, and high school is for grades Year 7–12. Secondary college is a name frequently used for high school. Tertiary education after high school is either at universities and TAFE (technical and further education) institutions.

In Australia, each school year starts in late January and finishes mid-December.

The legal drinking age in Australia is 18 years old.

AUSTUDY is financial help if you're 25 or older and studying or completing an Australian apprenticeship.